Heidi

Heidi

Johanna Spyri

Illustrations by Rozier-Gaudriault

Viking

Contents

1

UP THE MOUNTAIN

66 The pretty little Swiss town of Mayenfeld lies at the foot of a mountain range, whose grim rugged peaks tower high above the valley below.**99**

The pretty little Swiss town of Mayenfeld lies at the foot of a mountain range, whose grim rugged peaks tower high above the valley below. Behind the town a footpath winds gently up to the heights. The grass on the lower slopes is poor, but the air is fragrant with the scent of mountain flowers from the rich pasture land higher up.

One sunny June morning, a tall sturdy young woman was climbing up the path. She had a bundle in one hand and held a little girl about five years old by the other. The child's sunburned cheeks were flushed, which was not surprising, for though the sun was hot she was wrapped up as though it was midwinter. It was difficult

Building chalets—Swiss dwellings with wide, overhanging roofs—out of wood meant going into the forest and cutting logs during the great cold of winter. Once a tree was felled, the branches and trunk were brought down via mule tracks into the valley where they were prepared for use in construction.

7

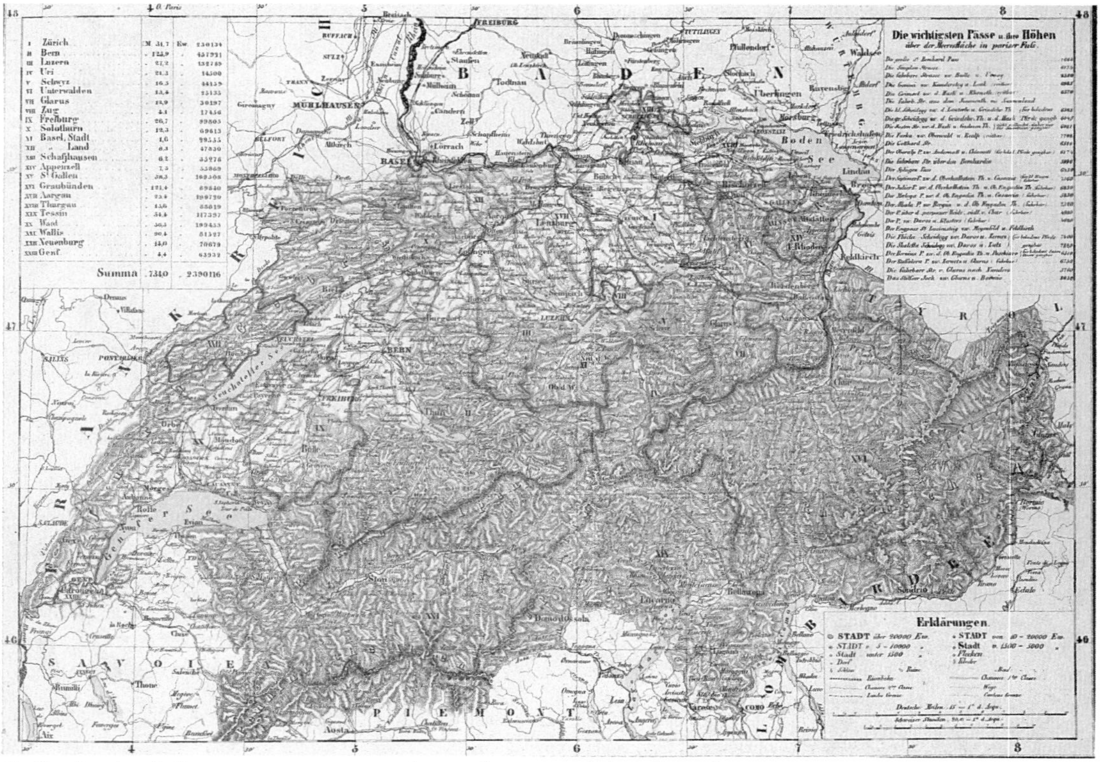
Die wichtigsten Pässe u. ihre Höhen
Erklärungen
BASEL
BERN
FREIBURG
MÜHLHAUSEN
Summa

Switzerland gets its name from Schwyz, which is the name of both a canton (something like a state in the U.S.) and a town at the very center of the country. During Heidi's time, there were twenty-two cantons, divided into nine large regions. Today there are twenty-three cantons.

to see what she was like for she was wearing two frocks, one on top of the other, and had a large red scarf wound round and round her as well. She looked like some shapeless bundle of clothing trudging uphill on a pair of hobnailed boots.

After climbing for about an hour, they came to the little village of Dörfli, halfway up the mountain. This was the woman's old home, and people called to her from their houses all the way up the street. She did not say much in reply but went on her way without stopping until she reached the last house. There a voice from within hailed her. "Half a minute, Detie," it said. "I'll come with you, if you're going any farther."

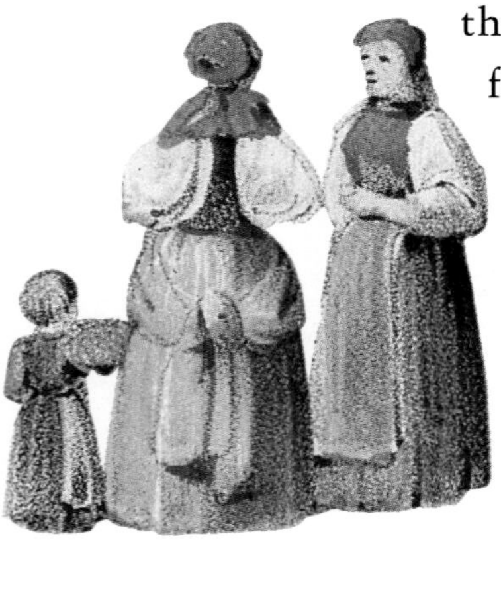

Detie stood still, but the little girl slipped her

hand free and sat down on the ground.

"Tired, Heidi?" Detie asked her.

"No, but I'm very hot," the child replied.

"We'll soon be there. Just keep going, and see what long strides you can take, and we'll arrive in another hour."

At that moment a plump, pleasant-faced woman came out of the house and joined them. The little girl got up and followed as the two grown-ups went ahead, gossiping hard about people who lived in Dörfli or round about.

"Where are you going with the child, Detie?" the village woman asked after a while. "I suppose she's the orphan your sister left?"

"That's right," Detie replied. "I'm taking her up to Uncle. She'll have to stay with him now."

"What, stay with Uncle Alp on the mountain? You must be crazy! How can you think of such a thing? But of course he'll soon send you about your business if you suggest that to him."

"Why should he? He's her grandfather and it's high time he did something for her. I've looked after her up to now, but I don't mind telling you, I'm not going to turn down a good job like the one I've just been offered, because of her. Her grandfather must do his duty."

"If he were like other people that might be all right," retorted Barbie, "but you know what he is. What does he know about looking after a child, and such a young one too? She'll never stand the life up there. Where's this job you're after?"

"In Germany," said Detie. "A wonderful job with a

good family in Frankfurt. Last summer they stayed in the hotel at Ragaz where I've been working as chambermaid. They had rooms on the floor I look after. They wanted to take me back with them then, but I couldn't get away. Now they've come back and have asked me again. This time I'm certainly going."

"Well, I'm glad I'm not that poor child," said Barbie, throwing up her hands in dismay. "Nobody really knows what's the matter with that old man, but he won't have anything to do with anybody, and he hasn't set foot in a church for years. When he does come down from the mountain, with his big stick in his hand—and that doesn't happen often—everybody scuttles out of his way. They're all scared stiff of him. He looks so wild with those bristling gray eyebrows and that dreadful beard. He's not the sort of person one would want to meet alone on the mountain."

"That's as may be, but he's got to look after his grandchild now, and if she comes to any harm that'll be his fault, not mine."

"I wonder what he's got on his conscience to make him live all alone up there, and hardly ever show his face," Barbie wondered. "There are all sorts of rumors, but I expect you know the whole story. Your sister must have told you plenty about him, didn't she?"

"Yes, she did, but I'm not telling. If he heard I'd been talking about him, I should catch it all right."

But Barbie did not mean to lose this excellent opportunity of getting to know more about the old man. She came from Prättigau, farther down the valley, and had only lived in Dörfli a short while, just since her marriage, so she still had much to learn about her neighbors. She was very anxious to know why the old man lived up on the mountain like a hermit, and why people were reluctant to talk about him as they did, freely enough, about everyone else. They didn't approve of him, that much was certain, but they seemed afraid to say anything against him. And then, why was he always called "Uncle Alp"? He couldn't be uncle to everyone in the village, but no one ever called him anything else; even Barbie used that name too. And here was her friend

With high glacial peaks all around them, mountain villages are often built in the shelter of a small valley, where the temperatures are milder and the winds not so fierce. Also, plants benefit from the water that collects when the snows melt.

Here, a scene from village life: this young couple has just been married, and is leading the way to the wedding feast.

Detie, who was related to him and had lived all her life in Dörfli, until a year ago. Then her mother had died, and she had found a good job in a big hotel at Ragaz. She had come from there that morning with Heidi, with the help of a lift on a hay cart as far as Mayenfeld.

Graübunden is a region in southeastern Switzerland, on the Italian border. The climate is dry and sunny. Livestock is raised at high altitudes, and the villages are often perched high in the mountains. The natives of Graübunden speak a simple form of Latin, close to Italian. *Above:* This pair is wearing the traditional garb.

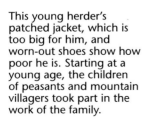

This young herder's patched jacket, which is too big for him, and worn-out shoes show how poor he is. Starting at a young age, the children of peasants and mountain villagers took part in the work of the family.

Now Barbie took her arm, and said coaxingly, "You could at least tell me how much of what they say is true, and how much only gossip. Come on now, do explain why he's so against everyone, and why everyone is afraid of him. Has he always been like that?"

"That I can't say for certain. I'm only twenty-six and he must be seventy or more, so I never knew him in his young days. All the same, if I could be sure that you wouldn't pass it on to everyone in Prättigau, I could tell you plenty about him. He and my mother both came from Domleschg."

"Go on, Detie, what do you take me for?" protested Barbie, half offended. "We aren't such gossips as all that in Prättigau, and anyway I'm quite capable of holding my tongue when I want to. Do tell me. I promise not to pass it on."

"All right then—but mind you keep your word!"

Detie glanced round to make sure that Heidi was not within earshot, but she was nowhere to be seen. She must have stopped following them some way back, and they had been too busy talking to notice. Detie stood still and looked in all directions. The path twisted and zigzagged down the mountainside, but she could see down it almost as far as Dörfli and there was nobody in sight anywhere along it.

"Ah, there she is," cried Barbie suddenly, "can't you see her?" She pointed to a little figure far below. "Look, she's climbing up the slopes with Peter and his goats. I wonder why he's taking them up so late today. Well, he'll keep an eye on her all right and you can get on with your story."

"Peter needn't bother himself," said Detie. "She can look after herself, though she's only five. She's got all her wits about her. She knows how to make the best of things too, which is just as well, seeing that the old man's got nothing now but his hut and two goats."

"I suppose he was better off once?" asked Barbie.

"I should just think he was. Why, he had one of the best farms in Domleschg. He was the elder son, with one brother, a quiet respectable fellow. But old Uncle wanted nothing but to ape the gentry and travel about all over the place. He got into bad company, and drank and gambled away the whole property. His poor parents died, literally died, of shame and grief when they heard of it. His brother was ruined too, of course. He took himself off, dear knows where, and nobody ever heard of him again. Uncle disappeared too. He had nothing left but a bad name. No one knew where he'd gone to, but after a while it came out that he had joined the army and was in Naples. Then no more was heard of him for twelve or fifteen years." Detie was enjoying herself.

"Go on," Barbie cried breathlessly.

"Well, one day he suddenly

In mountain and forest areas, woodworking was one of the most widespread and well-paid trades. Wood was the basic raw material for construction, and was also used to make many household objects and utensils: furniture, tableware, clogs, and so on. There were no machines in a carpenter's workshop during Heidi's time, but there were many tools, and knowing how to handle them surely and accurately was a valuable skill. An established carpenter would often accept young apprentices, who hoped to learn from him the craft of woodworking and the proper handling of saws, planes, and chisels.

Built of notched logs, granaries were set on stilts and were used to store mostly grain and cheese.

Newborns were frequently cared for by a woman who, after having a child, also nursed the children of others. The first part of a child's life was often counted in terms of "nursemaid's months."

reappeared in Domleschg with a young son, and wanted some of his relations to look after the boy. But he found all doors closed against him. Nobody wanted to have anything to do with him."

"Whew!" came in a whistle from Barbie.

"He was so angry he vowed he would never set foot in the place again. So he came to Dörfli and settled down there with the boy, who was called Tobias. People thought he must have met and married his wife down in the south. Apparently she died soon afterwards, though nothing is known for certain. He had saved a little money, enough to apprentice his boy to a carpenter. Tobias was a good sort and everyone in the village liked him—but no one trusted the old man! It was said that he had deserted from the army at Naples, so as to avoid some trouble about killing a man—not in battle, you understand, but in a brawl. All the same we accepted him as a member of the family. His grandmother and my mother's grandmother were sisters, so we called him Uncle, and as we're related to almost everyone in Dörfli, one way or another, the whole village soon called him Uncle too. Then, when he went to live right up there on the mountain, it became Uncle Alp."

"And what happened to Tobias?" Barbie asked eagerly.

"Give me a chance! I was just coming to that," Detie snapped at her. "Tobias was apprenticed to a carpenter in Mels, but as soon as he had learned his trade, he came home to Dörfli and married my sister Adelheid. They had always been fond of each other. They settled down very happily together as man and wife, but that didn't last long.

Only two years later he was killed by a falling beam while he was helping to build a house. Poor Adelheid got such a shock when she saw him carried home like that, that she fell ill with a fever, and never walked again. She had not been very strong before and used to have queer turns when it was hard to tell whether she was asleep or awake. She only survived him by a few weeks. That set tongues wagging of course. People said it was Uncle's punishment for his misspent life. They told him so to his face, and the pastor told him he ought to do penance to clear his conscience. That made him more angry than ever, and morose too. He wouldn't speak to anyone after the pastor's visit, and his neighbors began to keep out of his way. Then one day we heard that he'd gone to live up on the mountain and wasn't coming down any more. He's actually stayed up there from that day to this, at odds with God and man, as they say. My mother and I took Adelheid's baby girl to live with us. She was only about a year old when she was left an orphan. Then, when mother died last summer I wanted to get a job in the town, so I took Heidi up to Pfäffersdorf and asked old Ursula to look after her. I managed to get work in the town right through the winter, as I'm handy with my needle and there was always someone who wanted sewing or mending done. Then early this year that family from Frankfurt came again, the people I waited on last year; and now, as I told you, they want me to go back with them, and they're leaving the day after tomorrow. It's a first-rate job, I can tell you."

Lace makers crafted their delicately designed open-work fabric either by hand, using a needle to make each stitch, or with the help of a small portable loom.

During the seasonal migrations of the herds, certain high pastures became way stations between the lowland winter grazing grounds and the high alpine meadows above. The animals would stop to graze there either before going on toward the summits or when returning to the plains. Chalets would be built at these way stations, and shepherds stayed there during their stopovers.

Made of light wood and strips of metal, sleds were the perfect way to transport people and goods in a snow-covered country. The curved side pieces are called runners. On ice or frozen snow, a sled can reach very high speeds, and the rider needs great skill to keep it from tipping over.

66 Peter was eleven, and every morning he went down to Dörfli to fetch the goats and drive them up to graze all day in the fragrant mountain meadows above. **99**

"And you're going to hand that child over to the old man, just like that? I'm surprised that you can even think of such a thing, Detie," Barbie told her reproachfully.

"Well, what else can I do?" demanded Detie angrily. "I've done my best for her all these years, but obviously I can't saddle myself with a five-year-old child on this job. Look, we're half way up to Uncle's now," she went on. "Where are you going, Barbie?"

"I want to see Peter's mother. She does spinning for me in the winter. So this is where I leave you. Good-bye, Detie, and good luck."

Detie stood watching as Barbie went toward a little brown wooden hut sheltering in a small hollow a few yards from the path. It was so dilapidated that it was a good thing that it got some protection from the full force of the mountain gales. Even so, it must have been wretched to live in, as all the doors and windows rattled every time the wind blew and its rotten old beams creaked and shook. If it had been built in a more exposed position, it would certainly have been blown down into the valley long ago.

This was Peter the goatherd's home. He was eleven, and every morning he went down to Dörfli to fetch the goats and drive them up to graze all day in the fragrant mountain meadows above. Then, in the evening, he brought them down again, leaping with them over the hillside almost as nimbly as they did. He always gave a shrill whistle through his fingers when he reached the village so that the owners could come and collect their animals. It was usually children who answered the call—not even the youngest was afraid of these gentle goats.

During the summer months this was the only chance Peter had of seeing other boys and girls. For the rest of the time, goats were his only companions. He spent very little time at home with his mother and his old blind grandmother who lived with them. He used to leave the hut very early, after bolting his breakfast of a piece of bread and a mug of milk, and he always stayed as long as possible with the children in Dörfli, so he only got back in time to gobble his supper and tumble straight into bed. His father had been the goatherd before him, but he had been killed several years ago, when felling a tree. His mother's name was Bridget, but she was seldom called anything but "the goatherd's mother," and his grandmother was just Grannie to everyone, old and young alike.

For several minutes after Barbie had left her, Detie looked anxiously about for the two children with the goats, but there was no sign of them. She climbed a little

The evergreen trees we associate with the high mountains comprise a wide variety of species, and the wood of each has its particular use. The Norway spruce, widely used as a Christmas tree, has dense wood, which is used for building and for making musical instruments. The European silver fir, with its light-colored wood, is used in building and cabinetmaking. The larch with its rough bark is ideal for making posts and fencing. The Colorado spruce and the balsam fir of Canada, although hardy, sweet-scented, and attractive, offer wood of poor quality; they are more suitable for decorative uses.

Alpine goats are so sure-footed on steep rocky slopes that they are often used as guides for leading flocks of sheep up to the alpine meadows.

farther up the path to get a better view and then stopped to look again. She was getting very impatient.

The children had strayed far away from the path, for Peter always went his own way up the mountain. What mattered was where his goats would find the best bushes and shrubs to nibble. At first Heidi had scrambled up after him, puffing and panting, for her load of clothes made climbing hard, hot work. She did not complain, but she looked enviously at Peter, running about so freely on bare feet, in comfortable trousers; and at the goats whose nimble little legs carried them so lightly up the steep slopes and over bushes and stones. Then suddenly she sat down and pulled off her boots and stockings. She unwound the thick red scarf and quickly unbuttoned her best dress, which Detie had made her wear on top of her everyday one, to save carrying it. She took off both dresses and stood there in nothing but a little petticoat, waving her bare arms in the air with delight. Then she laid all the clothes together in a neat pile and danced off to catch up with Peter and the goats. He had not noticed what she was doing, and when he caught sight of her running toward him like that, he smiled broadly. He looked back and saw the pile of clothing she had left on the grass, and grinned from ear to ear, but he said nothing. Heidi felt much happier, and free as air, and began to chatter away, asking him a string of questions. He had to tell her how many goats he had, where he was taking them, and what he was going to do when he got there. Presently they reached the hut and came within Detie's view. As soon as she spotted them she called out shrilly:

"What on earth have you been doing, Heidi? What a sight you look! What have you done with your frocks? And the scarf? And those good new boots I bought you to come up here in, and the stockings I knitted for you? Wherever have you left them all?"

Heidi calmly pointed to the place where she had undressed. "There they are," she said. Her aunt could see something lying there, with a red spot on top, which was the scarf.

While girls looked for employment in the valleys, boys went into the mountains: they became shepherds or goatherds at a very early age.

"Oh, you naughty little thing!" she cried crossly. "What on earth made you take your clothes off like that? What's the meaning of it?"

"I didn't need them," replied Heidi, as if that were quite sufficient explanation.

"You stupid child, haven't you any sense at all?" scolded Detie. "And who do you think is going down to fetch them for you now? It would take me a good half hour. Peter, you run back and get them for me, and be quick about it. Don't stand there gaping, as if you were rooted to the ground."

"I'm late as it is," said Peter. He made no attempt to move but stood with his hands in his pockets as he had done all the time Detie had been shouting at Heidi.

"Well, you won't get very far, if you just stand there, staring," said Detie. "Look here's something for you." She made her tone more persuasive, and held out a bright new coin. The sight of this stirred him to action, and he dashed off with giant strides down the steep slope. He snatched up the pile of clothes and was back with them in no time. Detie had to admit that he had earned his reward. He tucked the coin away, deep down

Extremely steep paths can wind along the rocky face of a narrow gorge. Often blocked or damaged by rockfall after a thaw, they must be cleared and rebuilt by the mountain people who use them.

❝ Three old fir trees with huge branches stood behind the little house.**❞**

in his pocket, with a very broad grin, for such riches did not often come his way.

"Now you carry the things up to Uncle's for me. You're going that way I know." And Detie began to climb the steep path behind the goatherd's hut.

Peter was quite willing and followed on her heels, holding the bundle under his left arm and swinging the stick he used for the goats in his right hand. It took nearly an hour to reach the high pasture where Uncle Alp's hut stood on a little plateau. The little house was exposed to every wind that blew, but it also caught all the sunlight and commanded a glorious view right down the valley. Three old fir trees with huge branches stood behind it. Beyond them the ground rose steeply to the top of the mountain. There was rich grazing land immediately above the hut, but then came a mass of tangled undergrowth, leading to bare and rugged peaks.

Uncle Alp had made a wooden seat and fixed it to the side of the hut looking over the valley. Here he was sitting peacefully, with his pipe in his mouth and his hands on his knees as the little party approached. Peter and Heidi ran ahead of Detie for the last part of the way, and Heidi was actually the first to reach the old man. She went straight up to him and held out her hand. "Hello, Grandfather," she said.

"Hey, what's that?" he exclaimed gruffly, staring searchingly at her as he took her hand. She stared back, fascinated by the strange-looking old man, with his long beard and bushy gray eyebrows. Meanwhile Detie came toward them, while Peter stood watching to see what would happen.

"Good morning, Uncle," said Detie. "I've brought you Tobias's daughter. I don't suppose you recognize her as you haven't seen her since she was a year old."

"Why have you brought her here?" he demanded roughly. "And you be off with your goats," he added to Peter. "You're late, and don't forget mine." The old man gave him such a look that Peter disappeared at once.

"She's come to stay with you, Uncle," Detie told him, coming straight to the point. "I've done all I can for her these four years. Now it's your turn."

"My turn, is it?" snapped the old man, glaring at her. "And when she starts to cry and fret for you, as she's sure to do, what am I supposed to do then?"

"That's your affair," retorted Detie. "Nobody told me how to set about it when she was left on my hands, a baby barely a year old. Goodness knows I had enough to do already, looking after Mother and myself. But now I've got to go away to a job. You're the child's nearest relative. If you can't have her here, do what you like with her. But you'll have to answer for it if she comes to any harm, and I shouldn't think you'd want anything more on your conscience."

The houses in the high valleys are usually built on flat ground called glacial terraces or moraines. The villages are formed of houses clustered tightly together. Because the climate is so harsh, good relations among community members help everyone make it through the long winters.

To protect them from avalanches, mountain hamlets are often situated at the foot of a rocky spur, where several valleys come together. The streets between the houses are of packed earth edged with large flat stones, and domestic animals wander there freely. The communal structures—the school, the fountain, and the gathering hall—are grouped at the center of the village.

Detie was really far from easy in her mind about what she was doing, which was why she spoke so disagreeably, and she had already said more than she meant to.

The old man got up at her last words. She was quite frightened by the way he looked at her, and took a few steps backward.

"Go back where you came from and don't come here again in a hurry," he said angrily, raising his arm.

Detie didn't wait to be told twice. "Good-bye, then," she said quickly. "Good-bye, Heidi," and she ran off down the mountain, not stopping till she came to Dörfli. Here even more people called out to her than before, wanting to know what she had done with the child, whom they all knew.

"Where's Heidi? What have you done with Heidi?" they cried from their doorways and windows.

Detie replied, more reluctantly each time, "She's up at Uncle Alp's. Yes, that's what I said. She's with Uncle Alp." It made her uneasy to hear the women call back to her, from all sides, "How could you do it, Detie!" "Poor little mite!" "Fancy leaving that helpless little creature up there with that man!" Detie was thankful when she was out of earshot. She did not want to think about what she had done, for when her mother was dying, she had made Detie promise to look after the child. She comforted herself with the thought that she would be better able to do so if she took this job where she could earn good money, and hurried away as fast as she could from all those people who would try to make her change her mind.

66 As soon as Detie had
disappeared, the old man
sat down again on the
bench. 99

2

AT GRANDFATHER'S

As soon as Detie had disappeared, the old man sat
down again on the bench. He stared at the ground
in silence, blowing great clouds of smoke from his
pipe, while Heidi explored her new surroundings
with delight. She went up to the goat stall which
was built on to the side of the hut, but found it
empty. Then she went round to the back and stood for
a while listening to the noise the wind made whistling
through the branches of the old fir trees. Presently it
died down, and she came back to the front of the hut,

Pipes could be made of
clay, porcelain, or meer-
schaum (a fine white clay-
like mineral), or carved
from rosewood, boxwood,
cherry, or briar root. The
bowl was sometimes dec-
orated with figures or
designs. *Above*, two fancy
pipes from the nineteenth
century.

The inside of a mountain chalet during Heidi's time was built entirely of wood. As a building material, wood is dry and provides good insulation, holding in the heat from the fireplace. The mountaineers shown above are in traditional dress. The man and the boy are wearing knee pants, a woolen vest, and a coarse cotton shirt; the woman wears a long, tapering woolen dress, gathered at the bust with a long apron. Everyone wore wool stockings and either a cap or a hat. To the brim of his, the old shepherd has pinned an edelweiss flower—a small perennial herb that grows high in the Alps.

where she found her grandfather still sitting in the same position. As she stood watching him, hands behind her back, he looked up and said, "What do you want to do now?"

"I want to see what is inside the hut," she answered.

"Come on, then," he said, and he got up and led the way indoors. "Bring the bundle of clothes in with you," he added.

"I shan't want them any more," she declared.

The old man turned and looked sharply at her, and saw her black eyes shining with anticipation. "She's no fool," he muttered to himself, and added aloud, "Why's that?"

"I want to be able to run about like the goats do."

"Well, so you can," said her grandfather, "but bring the things inside all the same. They can go in the cupboard."

Heidi picked up the bundle and followed the old man into a biggish room which was the whole extent of his living quarters. She saw a table and a chair, and his bed over in one corner. Opposite that was a stove, over which a big pot was hanging. There was a door in one wall which the old man opened, and she saw it was a large cupboard with his clothes hanging in it. There were shelves in it too. One held his shirts, socks, and handkerchiefs, another plates, cups, and glasses, while on the top one were a round loaf, some smoked meat, and some cheese. Here, in fact, were all the old man's possessions. Heidi went inside the open cupboard and pushed her bundle right away to the back so that it would not easily be seen again.

"Where shall I sleep, Grandfather?" she asked next.

"Where you like," he replied.

This answer pleased Heidi, and as she was looking round the room for a good place she noticed a ladder propped against the wall near her grandfather's bed. She climbed up it at once and found herself in a hay loft. A pile of fresh, sweet-smelling hay lay there, and there was a round hole in the wall of the loft, through which she could see right down the valley.

Kitchen utensils were traditionally made of wood. This soup spoon was carved from walnut. The cauldron was an essential item of kitchen equipment: it was hung in the fireplace, where foods cooked slowly. These large pots were often made of cast bronze.

"I shall sleep up here," she called down. "It's a splendid place. Just come and see, Grandfather."

"I know it well," he called back.

"I'm going to make my bed now," she went on, "but you'll have to come up and bring me a sheet to lie on."

"All right," said her grandfather, and he went to the cupboard and searched among his belongings until he found a piece of coarse cloth, which he carried up to her. He found she had already made herself a sort of mattress and pillow of the hay, and had placed them so that she would be able to look through the hole in the wall when she was in bed.

"That's right," said the old man, "but it needs to be thicker than that," and he spread a lot more hay over hers so that she would not feel the hard floor through it. The thick cloth which he had brought for a sheet was so heavy that she

25

Above, a milking stool, made of fir. Its short, evenly spaced legs make it very stable.

The pail below, made of closely fitted wooden staves with a metal hoop fastened around them, was intended for collecting milk. The strainer, on the right, is perforated to allow cheese to drain.

could hardly lift it by herself, but its thickness made it a good protection against the prickly hay stalks. Together they spread it out, and Heidi tucked the ends under her "mattress" to make it all neat and comfortable. Then she looked at her bed thoughtfully for a moment, and said, "We've forgotten something, Grandfather."

"What's that?" he asked.

"A blanket to cover it, so that I can creep under it when I go to bed."

"That's what you think, is it? Suppose I haven't got one?"

"Oh, well then, it doesn't matter," said Heidi, "I can easily cover myself with hay," and she was just going to fetch some more when her grandfather stopped her. "Wait a bit," he said, and he went down the ladder, and took from his own bed a great sack made of heavy linen which he brought up to the loft.

"There, isn't that better than hay?" he asked, as they put it over the bed. Heidi was delighted with the result.

"That's a wonderful blanket, and my whole bed's lovely. I wish it was bedtime now so that I could get in it."

"I think we might have something to eat first, don't you?" said her grandfather. Heidi had forgotten everything else in her excitement over the bed, but at the mention of food, she realized how hungry she was, as she had eaten nothing all day except a piece of bread and a cup of weak coffee before setting out on her long journey. So she replied eagerly, "Oh, yes."

"Well then, if we are agreed, let us go and see about a meal," and he followed Heidi down the ladder. He went to the stove, lifted the big pot off the chain and put a smaller one in its place, then sat himself down on a three-legged stool and blew up the fire with the bellows till it was red and glowing. As the pot began to sing, he put a large piece of cheese on a toasting fork and moved it to and fro in front of the fire until it became golden yellow all over. At first Heidi just stood and watched with great interest, then she thought of something else and ran to the cupboard. When her grandfather brought the steaming pot and the toasted cheese to the table, he found it was laid with two plates, two knives, and the round loaf. Heidi had noticed these things in the cupboard and knew they would be needed for the meal.

"I'm glad to see you can think things out for yourself," he said, "but there is something missing."

Heidi looked at the steaming pot and went back to the cupboard. She could see one mug there and two glasses, so she took the mug and one of the glasses and put them on the table.

"That's right. You know how to be helpful," said her grandfather. "Now where are you going to sit?" He himself was in the only chair so Heidi fetched the three-legged stool and sat down on that.

"You've got a seat all right, but rather a low one, and even with my chair you would not be high enough

The blade of this finely sharpened knife is made of wrought iron. It fits perfectly onto the carved wooden handle.

This brightly colored pot, glazed and decorated with clover leaves, is a small milk pitcher.

A more primitive model than that on the opposite page, this type of milking stool was very common during Heidi's time. The feet are roughly carved and set into a rounded board of thick fir.

Here, the kitchen area in a chalet. Windows were small to keep the cold out. There was no chimney: smoke was left to seep out through the walls and roof. The lack of windows and the smoke often made a kitchen quite dark.

The cheese maker went from farm to farm helping families to make cheeses, such as big rounds of pressed cheese and farmer cheese (similar to cottage cheese). He sold his labor by the day and traveled with all his equipment: strainers, pots, skimmers, sieves, draining boards, and molds.

to reach the table." So saying, the old man got up and pushed his chair in front of Heidi's stool and put the mug filled with milk on it, and a plate on which was a slice of bread covered with the golden toasted cheese. "Now you have a table to yourself and can start to eat," he said. Then he perched himself on a corner of the big table and began his own meal.

Heidi took up the mug and drained it thirstily. After that she drew a deep breath—for she had been too busy drinking to breathe—and set the empty mug down.

"Is the milk good?" asked her grandfather.

"The best I've ever drunk," replied Heidi.

"You must have some more then," and he refilled her mug.

She ate her bread and cheese, which tasted delicious, and every now and then she took a drink. She looked as happy and contented as anyone could be.

After the meal her grandfather went to the goat stall and Heidi watched him sweep the floor with a broom and then put down fresh straw for the animals to sleep on. When that job was done he went into the shed, which was built on to the side of the hut, and sawed off several round sticks of wood. Then he bored holes to fit them in a strong flat piece of board, and when he had fitted them all together, the result was a high chair. Heidi watched him, silent in her amazement.

"Do you know what this is?" he asked, when he had finished.

"It's a chair specially for me," she said wonderingly. "And how quickly you made it!"

"She's got eyes in her head and knows how to use them," thought the old man. Next he busied himself with some small repairs in the hut, driving in a nail here and there, tightening a screw in the door and so on. Heidi followed at his heels, watching him with the closest attention, for everything was new and interesting to her.

Thus the afternoon passed. A strong wind sprang up again, whistling and rustling through the fir trees. The sound pleased Heidi so much that she began dancing and jumping about, and her grandfather stood watching her from the door of the shed. Suddenly there was a shrill whistle and Peter appeared in the midst of his herd of goats. Heidi gave a cry of delight

❝ A strong wind sprang up again, whistling and rustling through the fir trees. The sound pleased Heidi so much that she began dancing and jumping about.**❞**

and rushed to greet her friends of the morning. As the goats reached the hut they all stood still, except for two graceful animals, one brown and one white, which detached themselves from the others and went up to the old man. Then they began to lick his hands, for he was holding a little salt in them, as he did every evening to welcome them home.

Peter went away with the rest of the herd, and Heidi ran to the two goats and began to pat them gently. "Are these ours, Grandfather?" she asked. "Both of them? Do they go into the stall? Will they always be here with us?" Her questions followed so closely on each other that her grandfather could hardly

During the summer, the hay is cut twice in the mountains. First it is scythed and spread out to dry with a pitchfork, then turned over and gathered with a wooden rake.

get an answer in edgeways. When the goats had finished the salt, the old man said, "Now go and fetch your mug and the bread." She obeyed and was back in a flash. Then he filled her mug with milk from the white goat and gave it to her with a slice of bread. "Eat that and then go to bed," he said. "If you want a nightdress or anything like that, you'll find it in the bundle your aunt brought. Now I must see to the goats. Sleep well."

"Good night, Grandfather," she called, as he walked off with the animals. Then she ran after them to ask what the goats' names were.

"The white one is called Daisy and the brown Dusky," replied her grandfather.

"Good night Daisy, good night Dusky," called Heidi after the goats, who had disappeared into their stall. She ate her supper on the bench outside the hut. The wind was so strong, it almost blew her away, so she finished her bread and milk quickly and went indoors and up to bed. There she was soon sleeping as soundly as if she was tucked up in the finest bed in the world.

By selling as much milk, butter, and cheese as they could spare, a family was able to earn a little money to buy manufactured goods. This goatherd sells the milk of his goats on his way through the villages.

Her grandfather went to bed also before it was dark, for he always got up with the sun, and that came over the mountain tops very early in the summer. During the night the wind blew so hard that it shook the whole hut and made its beams creak. It shrieked down the chimney and brought one or two of the old fir trees' branches crashing down. So after a while the old man got up, thinking, "The child may be frightened."

He climbed up the ladder and went over to her bed. Just then the moon, which had been covered by scud-

66 She was fast asleep under her heavy coverlet. 99

ding clouds, shone straight through the hole in the wall onto Heidi's face. She was fast asleep under her heavy coverlet, one rosy cheek resting on her chubby little arm, and with such a happy expression on her face that she must surely have been dreaming of pleasant things. He stood looking down at her till clouds covered the moon again, darkening the room. Then he went back to bed.

66 It was very beautiful
on the mountain that
morning. 99

3

A DAY WITH THE GOATS

Heidi was awakened next morning by a shrill
whistle and as she opened her eyes a beam of sunlight
came through the hole in the wall, making the hay
shine like gold. At first she could not think where
she was, then she heard her grandfather's deep voice
outside and remembered joyfully that she had come
to live in the mountains. She had been glad to leave
old Ursula, who was very deaf and felt the cold so
much that she sat all day by the kitchen fire or the

33

Dressed up in his three-cornered hat, this goat-herd from the canton of Appenzell is going to market to sell his goat kids.

Edelweiss, an emblem of the high Alps, is a velvety plant that is cottony-soft, with a flower shaped like a star. Because it grows only at altitudes above 6,500 feet (2,000 meters), it can be difficult to find. Its rarity has made it a highly sought-after plant. Edelweiss means "noble white" in German.

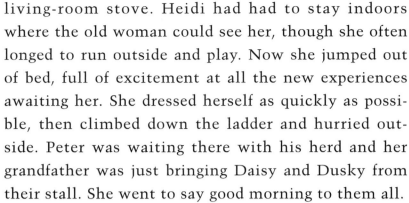

living-room stove. Heidi had had to stay indoors where the old woman could see her, though she often longed to run outside and play. Now she jumped out of bed, full of excitement at all the new experiences awaiting her. She dressed herself as quickly as possible, then climbed down the ladder and hurried outside. Peter was waiting there with his herd and her grandfather was just bringing Daisy and Dusky from their stall. She went to say good morning to them all.

"Do you want to go up to the pasture with Peter?" asked the old man. This idea clearly delighted her. "You must have a wash first, or the sun will laugh to see you look so black."

He pointed to a tub full of water, standing in the sun beside the door, and Heidi went over to it at once and began to splash about. Uncle Alp went indoors, calling to Peter, "Come here, General of the goats, and bring your knapsack with you." Peter held out the little bag which contained his meager lunch, and watched with big eyes as the old man put in a piece of bread and a piece of cheese, both twice as big as his own.

"Take this mug too, and fill it for her twice at dinnertime. She doesn't know how to drink straight from the goat as you do. She'll stay with you all day, and mind you look after her and see she doesn't fall down the ravine."

Heidi came running in. "The sun can't laugh at me now," she said. Her grandfather smilingly agreed. In her desire to please the sun, she had rubbed her face with the hard towel until she looked like a boiled lobster.

"When you come home tonight, you'll have to go right inside the tub like a fish, for you'll get black feet running about with the goats. Now off you go."

It was very beautiful on the mountain that morning. The night wind had blown all the clouds away and the sky was deep blue. The sun shone brilliantly on the green pasture land and on the flowers which were blooming everywhere. There were primroses, blue gentian, and dainty yellow rock-roses. Heidi rushed to and fro, wild with excitement at the sight of them. She quite forgot Peter and the goats, and kept stopping to gather flowers and put them in her apron. She wanted to take them home to stick among the hay in her bedroom, to make it look like a meadow.

Peter needed eyes all round his head. It was more than one pair could do to keep watch on Heidi as well as the goats, for they too were running about in all directions. He had to whistle and shout and swing his stick in the air to bring the wandering animals together.

"Where have you got to now, Heidi?" he called once rather crossly.

"Here," came her voice from behind a little hillock some distance back. It was covered with primulas which had a most delicious scent. Heidi had never smelled anything so lovely before and

Edelweiss has other names as well: lion's foot, snow immortal, silver star, star of the glaciers, starry cotton plant. More than thirty varieties exist in Asia, but only two grow in Europe. What look like white petals are really not part of the flower at all but are cottony leaves, or bracts. The real flowers, in the center, are so small that it takes a magnifying glass to see them.

Gentians, with their purple flowers, are used to make a medicinal tonic and a remedy for stomachache.

had sat down among them to enjoy it to the full.

"Come on," called Peter. "Uncle said I wasn't to let you fall over the ravine."

"Where's that?" she called, without moving.

"Right up above. We've still a long way to go, so do come on. Hear the old hawk croaking away up there?"

Heidi jumped up at this last remark and ran to him with her apron full of flowers.

"You've got enough now," he said, as they started to climb again. "Don't pick any more, otherwise you'll always be lagging behind, and besides, if you keep on, there won't be any left for tomorrow."

Heidi saw the sense of this, and anyway her apron was almost full. She kept close to Peter after that, and the goats went on in a more orderly fashion too, for now they could smell the fragrant herbs they loved which grew on their grazing ground, and were anxious to reach them.

Peter usually took up his quarters for the day at the very foot of a rocky mountain peak. On the steep slopes above, there were only a few bushes and stunted fir trees, and the summit itself was just bare rock. On one side was the sheer drop over the ravine which Uncle Alp had spoken of. When they reached this place Peter took off his knapsack and laid it, for safety, in a little hollow, for there were sometimes strong gusts of wind and he had no wish to see his precious food go bowling down the mountain. Then he lay down in the sun to rest after the strenuous climb. Heidi put her apronful of flowers in the same little hollow. Then she sat down beside Peter and looked around her. The valley below was bathed in sunlight. In front of them a snowclad mountain stood out against the blue sky and to the left of this was a huge mass of rock, with jagged twin peaks. Everything was very still. Only a gentle breeze set the blue and yellow flowers nodding on their slender stems.

Peter fell asleep and the goats climbed about among the bushes. Heidi sat quite still, enjoying it all. She gazed so intently at the mountain peaks that

Quick and fearless, the small goatlike antelopes called chamois live at altitudes between 2,500 and 10,000 feet (800 and 3,000 meters), but they can venture as high as 13,000 feet (4,000 meters). They are excellent climbers. The males are solitary wanderers; the females move in small groups, led by the eldest female.

Below, a stone bridge, with a tunnel and a narrow walkway built into the rock face on either side. Such structures made it possible to travel between villages in the high valleys.

The golden eagle, a large and powerful predator, captures live mammals and birds.

The chamois has vertical horns five to six inches (fourteen to seventeen centimeters) in height.

The legs of the golden eagle are covered with brown feathers. It has yellow, extraordinarily powerful claws that end in sharp points.

soon they seemed to her to have faces and to be looking at her like old friends. Suddenly she heard a loud noise. Looking up, she saw an enormous bird, circling overhead with outstretched wings and croaking harshly as it flew. "Peter, Peter, wake up!" she cried. "Here's the hawk." Peter sat up and together they watched as the great bird soared higher and higher into the sky and finally disappeared over the gray peaks.

"Where's it gone to?" asked Heidi, who had never seen a bird as big as that before and had watched its flight with great interest.

"Home to its nest," replied Peter.

"Does it live right up there? How wonderful! Why does it make such a noise?"

"Because it has to," explained Peter briefly.

"Let's climb up and see where it lives," she proposed.

"Oh, no, we won't! Even the goats can't climb as high as that, and don't forget Uncle told me to look after you," he said with marked disapproval. To Heidi's surprise he then began whistling and shouting, but the goats recognized the familiar sounds and came toward him from all directions, though some lingered to nibble a tasty blade of grass, while others butted one another playfully. Heidi jumped up and ran among them, delighted to see them so obviously enjoying themselves. She spoke to each one, and every one was different and easily distinguishable from the others.

Meanwhile Peter opened his bag and spread its

contents out in a square on the ground, two large portions for Heidi and two smaller ones for himself. Then he filled the mug with milk from Daisy and placed it in the middle of the square. He called to Heidi, but she was slower to come than the goats had been. She was so busy with her new playmates that she had ears and eyes for nothing else. He went on calling till his voice re-echoed from the rocks and at

66 She gazed so intently at the mountain peaks that soon they seemed to her to have faces.99

last she appeared. When she saw the meal laid out so invitingly, she skipped up and down with pleasure.

"Stop jigging about," said Peter, "it's dinnertime. Sit down and begin."

"Is the milk for me?"

"Yes, and those huge pieces of bread and cheese. I'll get you another mugful from Daisy when you've drunk that one. Then I'll have a drink myself."

"Where will you get yours from?" she inquired.

"From my own goat, Spot. Now start eating."

She drank the milk, but ate only a small piece of bread and passed the rest over to Peter, with the cheese. "You can have that," she said. "I've had enough." He looked at her with amazement for he had never in his life had any food to give away. At first he hesitated, thinking she must be joking, but she went on holding it out to him and finally put it on his knee. This convinced him that she really meant what she said, so he took it, nodded his thanks and settled down to enjoy the feast. Heidi meanwhile sat watching the goats.

"What are they all called, Peter?" she asked presently.

Peter did not know a great deal, but this was a question he could answer without difficulty. He told her all the names, pointing to each animal in turn. She listened attentively and soon knew one from the other. Each had little tricks by which it could easily be recognized by anyone looking at them closely, as she was doing. Big Turk had strong horns, and was always trying to butt the others, so

This young shepherd carries a wooden container full of milk hanging from a stick over his shoulder. When he came and went from the sheepfold to the village, he would act as a traveling vendor, supplying milk to the dairies and cheese producers in the mountains.

they kept out of his way as much as possible. The only one to answer him back was a frisky little kid called Finch, with sharp little horns, and Turk was generally too astonished at such impudence to make a fight of it. Heidi was particularly attracted to a little white goat called Snowflake, which was bleating most pitifully. She had tried earlier to comfort it. Now she ran up to it again, put her arm round its neck, and asked fondly, "What's the matter, Snowflake? What are you crying for?" At that, the

66 She drank the milk. **99**

goat nestled against her and stopped bleating.

Peter had not yet finished his meal, but he called out between mouthfuls, "She's crying because her mother doesn't come up here any more. She's been sold to someone in Mayenfeld."

"Where's her grandmother then?"

"Hasn't got one."

"Or her grandfather?"

"Hasn't one."

"Poor Snowflake," said Heidi, hugging the little animal again. "Don't cry any more. I shall be up here every day now, and you can always come to me if you feel lonely." Snowflake rubbed her head on the little girl's shoulder, and seemed to be comforted.

Peter had now finished eating, and came up to Heidi who was making fresh discoveries all the time. She noticed that Daisy and Dusky seemed more independent than the other goats and carried themselves with a sort of dignity. They led the way as the herd went up to the bushes again. Some of them stopped here and there to sample a tasty herb, others went straight up, leaping over any small obstacles in their path. Turk was up to his tricks as usual, but

66 The goat nestled against her and stopped bleating. **99**

Daisy and Dusky ignored him completely and were soon nibbling daintily at the leaves of the two thickest bushes. Heidi watched them for some time. Then she turned to Peter, who was lying full length on the grass.

"Daisy and Dusky are the prettiest of all the goats," she said.

"I know. That's Uncle—he keeps them very clean and gives them salt and he has a fine stall for them," he replied. Then he suddenly jumped up and ran after his herd, with Heidi close behind, anxious not to miss

A shepherd carries a young nanny goat over a treacherous part of the path homeward, and the rest of the herd will soon follow. Goats in the Alps are bred for their milk, which is used to make cheeses. Excellent milk producers, they must return from the steep pastures where they graze by day to be milked each evening.

anything. He had noticed that inquisitive little Finch was right at the edge of the ravine, where the ground fell away so steeply that if it went any farther, it might go over and would certainly break its legs. Peter stretched out his hands to catch hold of the little kid, but he slipped and fell, though he managed to grasp one of its legs and Finch, highly indignant at such treatment, struggled wildly to get away. "Heidi, come here," called Peter, "come and help."

He couldn't get up unless he let go of Finch's leg which he was nearly pulling out of its socket already. Heidi saw at once what to do, and pulled up a handful of grass which she held under Finch's nose.

"Come on, don't be silly," she said. "You don't want to fall down there and hurt yourself."

At that the little goat turned round and ate the

The goats wear bells around their necks so that when the flocks range freely over the high alpine meadows, the shepherd can know where they are. He must watch that they graze first on the lowest slopes so that they can ascend to the higher, cooler slopes when it is hottest.

66 Heidi saw at once what to do, and pulled up a handful of grass which she held under Finch's nose.**99**

grass from her hand, and Peter was able to get up. He took hold of the cord, on which a little bell was hung round Finch's neck. Heidi took hold of it too, on the other side, and together they brought the runaway safely back to the herd. Then Peter took up his stick to give it a good beating, and seeing what was coming, Finch tried to get out of the way.

"Don't beat him," pleaded Heidi. "See how frightened he is."

"He deserves it," Peter replied, raising his arm, but she caught hold of him and exclaimed, "No,

you're not to! It will hurt him. Leave him alone!" She looked at him so fiercely that he was astonished and dropped the stick.

"I won't beat him if you'll give me some of your cheese again tomorrow," he said, feeling he ought to have some compensation after the fright the little goat had given him.

"You can have it all, tomorrow and every day," promised Heidi, "I shan't want it. And I'll give you some of my bread as well, but then you must never beat Finch or Snowflake or any of them."

"It's all the same to me," said Peter, which was his way of saying that he promised. He let Finch go and it bounded back to the herd.

It was getting late and the setting sun spread a wonderful golden glow over the grass and the flowers, and the high peaks shone and sparkled. Heidi sat for a while, quietly enjoying the beautiful scene, then all at once she jumped up, crying, "Peter, Peter! A fire, a fire! The mountains are on fire, and the snow and the sky too. Look, the trees and the rocks are all burning, even up there by the hawk's nest. Everything's on fire!"

"It's always like this in the evening," Peter said calmly, whittling away at his stick. "It's not a fire."

"What is it then?" she cried, rushing about to look at the wonderful sight from all sides. "What is it, Peter?"

"It just happens," he said.

"Oh, just see, the mountains have got all rosy

The bronze bell on the left with the wide leather strap is intended for a cow. The one on the right, made of hammered bronze, is meant for a goat; the collar was carved from a single piece of bentwood.

During the winter, the sheep and goats stay inside a stable, eating the hay and grain stored for them earlier. In summer, the animals return to the high grazing grounds, stopping twice a year in the *mayens*, or meadows, lying below the high pastures.

red! Look at the one with the snow on it, and that one with the big rocks at the top. What are their names, Peter?"

"Mountains don't have names," he answered.

"How pretty the rosy snow looks, and the red rocks. Oh dear," she added, after a pause, "now the color's going and everything's turning gray. Oh, it's all over." She sat down, looking as upset as if it was indeed the end of everything.

"It'll be the same again tomorrow," explained Peter. "Now it's time to go home." He whistled and called the goats together and they started the downward journey.

"Is it always like this up here?" asked Heidi hopefully.

"Usually."

"Will it really be the same tomorrow?"

"Yes, it will," he assured her.

With this she was content and as she had so much to think about, she didn't say another word till they reached the hut and saw her grandfather sitting under the fir trees, on the seat he had fixed there so that he could watch for the return of his animals. The little girl ran toward him, followed by Daisy and Dusky, and Peter called, "Good night, Heidi. Come again tomorrow." She ran back to say good-bye and promised to go with him next day. Then she put her arms around Snowflake's neck and said, "Sleep well, Snowflake. Remember I'll be coming with you again tomorrow and you're not to cry any more." Snowflake gave her a trusting look and scampered off after the other goats.

The shepherds who kept watch over the flocks and milked them had a great deal of free time. Some spent it playing an instrument (such as the flute, reed pipe, or horn) or carving small statues and objects out of wood. Their diet was monotonous, consisting mostly of milk and cheese. When delivering milk to the village, the shepherds would bring back bread, vegetables, or other kinds of food.

"Oh, Grandfather," Heidi cried, as she ran back to him, "it was lovely up there, with all the flowers and then the fire and the rosy rocks. And see what I've brought you." She shook out the contents of her little apron in front of him, but the poor flowers had all faded and looked like so much hay. She was terribly upset.

"What's happened to them? They weren't like that when I picked them."

"They wanted to stay in the sun and didn't like being shut up in your apron," he explained.

"Then I'll never pick any more. Grandfather, why does the hawk croak so loudly?"

"You go and jump in the washtub, while I milk the goats," he replied. "Then we'll have supper

66 She shook out the
contents of her little
apron in front of him.**99**

together indoors and I'll tell you about the hawk."

As soon as Heidi was settled on her new high
chair with her grandfather beside her and a mug of
milk in front of her, she repeated her question.

"He's jeering at all the people who live in the villages down below and make trouble for one another.

You can imagine he's saying, 'If only you would all mind your own business and climb up to the mountain tops as I do, you'd be a lot better off.' The old man spoke these words so fiercely that it really reminded Heidi of the croaking of the great bird.

"Why haven't mountains got names?" she asked next.

"But they have," he told her, "and if you can describe one to me so that I can recognize it, I'll tell you its name."

Eagles and hawks hunt by flying low over the grasslands; their keen eyesight allows them to spot their victims easily. The speed and accuracy of their flight make them skillful predators.

So she told him about the mountain with the twin peaks and described it very well. Her grandfather looked pleased. "That's called Falkniss," he said. Then she described the one covered with snow and he told her its name was Scesaplana.

"You enjoyed yourself, then?" he asked.

"Oh yes," she cried, and told him all the wonderful things that had happened during the day. "The fire in the evening was the best of all. Peter said it wasn't a fire, but he couldn't tell me what it really was. You can though, Grandfather, can't you?"

"It's the sun's way of saying good night to the mountains," he explained. "He spreads that beautiful light over them so that they won't forget him till he comes back in the morning."

Heidi liked this explanation very much, and longed for another day to begin so that she could go up and watch the sun's good night again. But first she

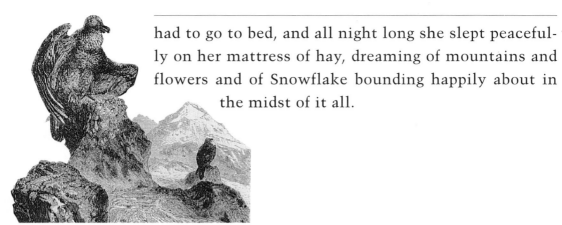

had to go to bed, and all night long she slept peaceful-ly on her mattress of hay, dreaming of mountains and flowers and of Snowflake bounding happily about in the midst of it all.

A rare bird, the lam-mergeier has an enor-mous wingspan and soars through the air with great elegance. It places its nest of branches and bone fragments on a ledge along a cliff.

4

A VISIT TO GRANNIE

Certain granaries, set on
short legs, were used by
both shepherds and by
mountain men. The loft
inside was divided into as
many compartments as
there were owners, and
usually held hay.

All through that summer Heidi went up to the pasture
every day with Peter and the goats, and grew brown as
a berry in the mountain sunshine. She grew strong
and healthy and was as happy and carefree as a bird in
her new life. But when autumn came, strong winds
began to blow, and her grandfather said to her, "Today
you must stay at home. A little thing like you might
easily get blown over the side of the mountain by a
gust of wind."

Peter was always very disappointed when Heidi could not go with him. He had grown so used to her company that he found it terribly dull to be by himself again, and of course he missed the good bread and cheese she always shared with him. The goats were twice as troublesome, too, when she was not there. They seemed to miss her and scattered all over the place, as though they were looking for her.

But Heidi was happy wherever she was. Of course she loved going up the mountain where there was always so much to see, but she also enjoyed going round with her grandfather, watching him at his carpentry and all the other jobs. She especially liked to see him make the goat's milk cheese. He rolled up his sleeves and plunged his arms deep into a big pot of milk which he stirred thoroughly with his hands until in due course he produced the delicious round cheeses. But what she liked most of all was the noise the wind made in the old fir trees. She often left what she was doing to go and stand under them with her face turned up, listening and watching the swaying branches as the wind whistled and whirled through them. The wind blew right through her too, though now that the weather was cooler she wore socks and shoes and put on a dress once more. That strange music in the tree tops had a special fascination for her and she could not stay indoors when she heard it.

All at once it turned really cold and Peter arrived in the mornings blowing on his hands to warm them. Then one night it started to snow and in the morning

Walking to midnight mass was a traditional part of Christmas in the Alpine countries. In the muffled silence of the snow-covered landscape, the sound of carols and Christmas music brought a touch of magic.

everything was white. It snowed until there was not a single green leaf to be seen, and of course Peter didn't bring the goats up. From the window Heidi watched with delight as the snowflakes fell, faster and faster, and the snow drifted higher and higher till the hut was buried up to the window sills and it was impossible to go out. She hoped it would go on falling until the hut was completely covered, so that they would have to light the lamp during the day, but that did not happen. Next morning her grandfather was able to dig his way out, and shovelled the snow away from

When the snow was deep, traveling became extremely dangerous. Horse-drawn carts, sleighs, and carriages could tip over because of the deep ruts already cut into the roads. Horses needed to be shod with special studded horse-shoes to keep their footing on patches of ice.

66 From the window Heidi watched with delight as the snowflakes fell, faster and faster. 99

the walls, throwing up great piles of it from his spade as he worked. Then in the afternoon he and Heidi sat down by the fire, each on a three-legged stool, for of course he had long ago made one for her. They were interrupted by a great banging at the door, as though someone was kicking it. Then it was opened, and there stood Peter, knocking the snow off his boots before coming in. He had had to fight his way through high drifts and it was so cold that the snow had frozen on to him, and still clung to his clothes. But he had kept bravely on, determined to get to Heidi after not seeing her for a whole week.

"Hullo," he said and went straight over to the stove. He didn't say anything more but stood beaming at them, well pleased to be there. Heidi watched in astonishment as the heat of the stove began to thaw the snow so that it trickled off him in a steady flow.

"Well, General," said the old man, "how are you getting on now that you've had to leave your army and start chewing a pencil?"

"Chewing a pencil?" exclaimed Heidi with interest.

"Yes, in the winter Peter has to go to school and learn to read and write. That's no easy matter you know, and it sometimes helps a bit to chew a pencil, doesn't it, General?"

Close inspection of this engraving reveals some of the teaching aids typically used in a primary school at that time: a compass, natural-history illustrations, pictures of landscapes, and busts of famous men. The schoolmaster is holding an abacus, which was used to teach counting. The desks have an attached bench and are built to accomodate inkwells and slates. The schoolchildren are dressed quite formally by today's standards.

"Yes it does," agreed Peter.

Immediately Heidi wanted to know just what he did at school. Peter always found it difficult to put his thoughts into words and Heidi had so many questions to ask that no sooner had he managed to deal with one than she was ready with two or three more, most of them needing a whole sentence in reply. His clothes were quite dry again before she was satisfied. The old man listened quietly to their chatter, smiling from time to time. As they fell silent he got up and went over to the cupboard.

After school lets out, it is time to play. When there is snow on the ground, nothing lets off steam like a snowball fight, especially if you've just sat for hours in a classroom. Here, some children have an all-out battle with a young chimney sweep, whose sooty figure stands starkly against the white winter landscape as he vigorously defends himself.

"Well, General, you've been under fire, now you'll need some refreshment," he said.

He soon had supper ready and Heidi put chairs round the table. The hut was less bare now than when she first arrived, for Grandfather had made one bench which was fixed to the wall and other seats big enough for two people, for Heidi always liked to be close beside him. Now they could all sit down in comfort, and as Peter did so, he opened his round eyes very wide at the huge piece of dried meat Uncle Alp put on a thick slice of bread for him. It was a long time since he had had such a good meal. As soon as they had finished eating Peter got ready to go, for it was growing dark.

"Good-bye," he said, "and thank you. I'll come again next Sunday, and Grannie says she would like you to come and see her."

Heidi was delighted at the idea of going to visit someone, for that would be something quite new, so the first thing she said next morning was, "Grandfather, I must go

and see Peter's Grannie today. She'll be expecting me."

"The snow is too deep," said Uncle Alp, trying to put her off.

But the idea was firmly in her head, and day after day she said at least half a dozen times that she really must go or Grannie would be tired of waiting for her. On the fourth day after Peter's visit the snow froze hard and crackled underfoot, and the sun was shining brightly, straight on to Heidi's face as she sat on her high chair eating her dinner. Again she said, "I must go and see Grannie today, or she'll think I'm not coming."

Her grandfather left the table and went up to the loft, from which he brought down the thick sack off her bed. "Come on, then," he said, and they went out together.

Heidi skipped delightedly into the shining white world. The branches of the fir trees were weighed down with snow which sparkled in the sunshine. Heidi had never seen anything like it.

"Just look at the trees," she cried, "they're all gold and silver."

Meanwhile Grandfather had dragged a big sledge out of the shed. It had a bar along one side to hold on to, and it was steered by pressing the heels against the ground on one side or the other. To please Heidi he went round with her to look at the snow-

Before they became fashionable recreational toys, sleds were a common means of getting about in Switzerland.

❝ They went down the mountain so fast that Heidi felt as though she was flying . . . ❞

clad trees. Then he sat down on the sledge with her on his knees, well wrapped up in the sack to keep her warm. He held her tightly with his left arm and, taking hold of the bar with his right hand, pushed off with both feet. They went down the mountain so fast that Heidi felt as though she was flying, and screamed with delight. They stopped with a jerk just outside Peter's hut. Grandfather set her on her feet and took off the sack.

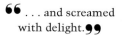

66 . . . and screamed with delight.99

"Now go in," he said, "but start for home as soon as it begins to get dark." Then he turned back up the mountain, pulling the sledge behind him.

The door Heidi opened led into a small kitchen, in which there was a stove and some pots on a shelf. A second door opened into another low little room. Compared with Grandfather's hut with its fine big room and the hay loft above, this place seemed wretchedly cramped. She went in and saw a woman sitting at a table mending a jacket which she recognized as Peter's. In one corner another woman, old and bent, was spinning. Heidi went straight to her and said, "Hullo, Grannie, here I am at last. I expect you thought I was never coming."

Grannie raised her head and felt for Heidi's hand. When she had found it, she held it in her own for a while and then said, "Are you the child from Uncle Alp's? Are you Heidi?"

Sleds were made by a cabinetmaker or cooper. The little sled shown here was designed to be handled by even the youngest children. It has curved runners made of bentwood and reinforced by iron rods, and can go very fast on snowy slopes.

Swiss chalets' sturdy, square frames, wooden staircases, balustrades, and gently sloping roofs make them ideal mountain dwellings.

The traditional Swiss cap for females was made of light cloth or velvet, trimmed with richly embroidered ribbons carrying images of mountain flowers.

"Yes, and Grandfather has just brought me down on the sledge."

"Fancy that. And yet your hand is so warm. Bridget, did Uncle Alp really bring her himself?"

Peter's mother left her mending to come and look at the child. "I don't know, mother," she said, "it does not sound likely. She must be mistaken."

Heidi looked her straight in the eye and said firmly, "I'm not mistaken. It was Grandfather. He wrapped me up in my blanket and brought me down himself."

"Well, well. Peter must have been right after all in what he told us about Uncle Alp," said Grannie. "We always thought he'd got it all wrong. Who would have believed it? To tell the truth, I didn't think the child would last three weeks up there. What does she look like, Bridget?"

"She's thin, like her mother was, but she's got black eyes and curly hair like Tobias and the old man. She's really more like them, I think."

Heidi looked about the room while the women were talking, and her sharp eyes missed nothing.

"One of your shutters is hanging loose, Grannie," she remarked. "Grandfather would soon mend it, and it'll break the window if nothing's done about it. Look how it bangs to and fro."

"I can't see it, my dear, but I can hear it very well, and everything else that creaks and clatters here when the wind blows through the cracks. The place is falling to pieces and at night, when the other two are asleep, I am often afraid that some time it may fall on us and kill us all. And there's no one to do anything about it. Peter doesn't know how."

"Why can't you see the shutter?" asked Heidi, pointing. "Look, there it goes again."

"I can't see at all, child, it's not only the shutter," said the old woman with a sigh.

"If I go out and pull the shutter right back so that it's really light in here, you'll be able to see, won't you?"

"No, not even then, light or dark makes no difference to me."

"But if you come out in the shining white snow, I'm sure you'll see then. Come and see." Heidi took the old woman's hand and tried to pull her up, for she was very upset at the thought of her never seeing anything.

"Let me be, child. I can't see any better even in the light of the snow. I'm always in the dark."

"Even in summer, Grannie?" Heidi persisted anxiously. "Surely you can see the sunshine and watch it say good night to the mountains and make them all red like fire. Can't you?"

"No, child, nor that either. I shall never see them again."

Heidi burst into tears.

In the villages like the one in *Heidi*, the women organized a big laundry day once a season. When wood ashes are combined with hot water, they make lye, which is an ingredient of soap. So ashes from the fireplace had been carefully saved, and on the night before wash day, the clothes were set in a large tub to soak. The next morning, the clothes were piled into another tub, this one with a faucet, and covered with the ashes. Boiling water was poured over them and drained off through the faucet. The women would then boil the water again and continue to perform the operation as many times as necessary. Then the laundry was brought to the village fountain where it was scrubbed on a large board and rinsed in several changes of water. The women carefully cleaned the fountain's basin before washing laundry in it.

This pail, made of closely fitted boards held by a hoop, was used for preparing food. The bowl, with its two small wooden handles, served as a soup plate.

This shepherd's table, carved of larch and fir, has only one leg at each end. This allowed the two benches set out on either side at meal times to fit back underneath it afterward.

"Can't anyone make you see?" she sobbed. "Isn't there anyone who can?"

For some time Grannie tried in vain to comfort her. Heidi hardly ever cried, but when she did it was always difficult to make her stop. The old woman got quite worried and at last she said, "Come here, my dear, and listen to me. I can't see, but I can hear, and when one is blind, it is so good to hear a friendly voice, and yours I love already. Come and sit beside me and tell me what you and Grandfather do up on the mountain. I used to know him well, but I haven't heard anything of him for years, except what Peter tells us—and that's not much."

Heidi dried her tears. She saw a ray of hope. "Just wait till I tell Grandfather about you. He'll be able to make you see, and he'll mend the hut too. He can do anything."

Grannie did not contradict her, and Heidi began to chatter away telling everything she did up there, both in summer and in winter. She told how clever Grandfather was at making things, how he had made stools and chairs and new mangers for the goats, and even a bath tub, and a milk bowl, yes, and spoons—all out of wood. Grannie understood from her voice how eagerly she must have watched him at work.

"I'd like to be able to make things like that myself one day," Heidi ended up.

"Did you hear that, Bridget?" Grannie asked her daughter. "Fancy Uncle doing all that!"

Suddenly the outer door banged and Peter burst into the room. He pulled up short and stared when he saw Heidi, then gave a very friendly grin as she greeted him.

"What, back from school already?" asked Grannie. "It's years since I've known an afternoon pass so quickly. Well Peterkin, how are you getting on with your reading?"

"Just the same," he replied.

"Oh dear," she sighed, "I hoped you might have something different to tell me by now. You'll be twelve in February."

"What to tell you? What do you mean?" asked Heidi, all interest.

"Only that perhaps he'd learned to read at last. There's an old prayer book up on the shelf, with some beautiful hymns in it. I haven't heard them for a very long time and can't repeat them any more to myself. I keep hoping Peterkin will be able to read them to me. But he doesn't seem able to learn. It's too difficult for him."

"I think I must light the lamp," said Bridget, who had been darning all this while. "The afternoon has passed so

Top, a wooden laundry tub. Below it is a ladle, also made of wood. Soup was a daily staple of the mountain people's diet, and so ladles were one of the most common kitchen utensils.

This box bed of carved wood has a sliding door to keep the heat in. It was very cozy on cold winter nights!

Christmas carols are among the best-known religious hymns. For many people they are a significant part of holiday festivities.

This mountaineer from the canton of Appenzell is dressed in his holiday clothes. He is wearing a cloth cap with a pom-pom, an embroidered vest, loose-fitting trousers with a high belt, and a white shirt.

quickly I hadn't noticed it was getting dark."

Heidi jumped up at that. "If it's getting dark I must go," she cried. "Good-bye Grannie." She said good-bye to the others and was just leaving when Grannie called anxiously, "Wait a minute, Heidi, you can't go alone. Peter will come with you and see you don't fall. And don't stand about and let her get cold. Has she something warm to put on?"

"No, I haven't," Heidi called back, "but I shan't be cold," and she ran off so fast that Peter could hardly keep pace with her.

"Bridget, take my shawl and run after her," cried Grannie in distress, "she'll freeze to death in this bitter cold," and Bridget took it and went after them. But the children had only gone a very little way up the mountain when they saw Uncle Alp striding toward them, and almost at once they were together.

"Good girl, you did as you were told," he said. Then he wrapped her in the sack again, picked her up in his arms, and turned for home. Bridget was just in time to see what happened, and she went back indoors with Peter to describe the surprising sight to her mother.

"Thank God the child is all right," exclaimed the old woman. "I hope Uncle Alp will let her come to see me again. Her visit has done me a deal of good. What a kind heart the little one has and how pleasantly she chatters." Grannie was in very good spirits. "I hope she comes again," she said several times that evening, "it would be something to look forward to."

"Yes, indeed," agreed Bridget each time, while

Peter grinned broadly, and said, "Told you so."

And out on the mountain Heidi was chattering away inside the sack to her grandfather, though he couldn't hear a word through its eightfold thickness.

"Wait till we're home and then tell me," he said.

As soon as they were indoors and Heidi had been unwrapped she began, "Tomorrow we must take a hammer and some big nails down to Peter's house, so that you can mend Grannie's shutter and lots of other things too, because her whole house creaks and rattles."

"Oh, we must, must we? Who told you to say that?"

66 He picked her up in his arms, and turned for home. **99**

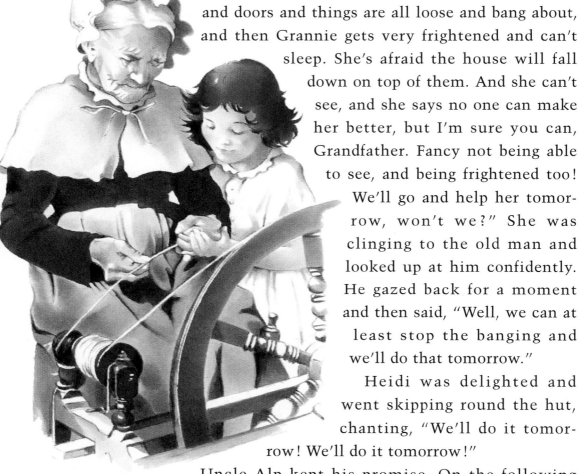

"Nobody told me. I just know. The shutters and doors and things are all loose and bang about, and then Grannie gets very frightened and can't sleep. She's afraid the house will fall down on top of them. And she can't see, and she says no one can make her better, but I'm sure you can, Grandfather. Fancy not being able to see, and being frightened too! We'll go and help her tomorrow, won't we?" She was clinging to the old man and looked up at him confidently. He gazed back for a moment and then said, "Well, we can at least stop the banging and we'll do that tomorrow."

Heidi was delighted and went skipping round the hut, chanting, "We'll do it tomorrow! We'll do it tomorrow!"

❝ Heidi ran to her and pulled up a little stool beside her, sat down and began to chatter away.**❞**

Uncle Alp kept his promise. On the following afternoon they went down on the sledge again and Heidi was set down outside the cottage. "Go in now," he said, as before, "but come away when it begins to get dark." Then he laid Heidi's sack on the sledge and disappeared round the side of the building.

Heidi had hardly set foot inside the door before Grannie called out from her corner, "Here she comes again!" She stopped spinning and held out both hands. Heidi ran to her and pulled up a little stool beside her, sat down and began to chatter away. Suddenly there came a series of loud bangs on the wall which so startled Grannie that she almost knocked her spinning wheel over.

"This time the place is really falling down," she cried tremulously. Heidi took hold of her arm and said, "Don't be afraid, Grannie. That's only Grandfather with his hammer. He's mending everything so that you won't be frightened any more."

"Is it true? God has not forgotten us after all. Can you hear it, Bridget? It really does sound like a hammer. Go out and see who it is, and if it's Uncle Alp ask him to come in so that I can thank him."

It was Uncle Alp of course. Bridget found him nailing a wedge-shaped piece of wood on to the wall. "Good day, Uncle," she said. "Mother and I are grateful to you for helping us like this, and Mother would like to thank you herself if you'll step inside. I'm sure no one else would have done as much for us and we won't forget it . . ."

But he interrupted her roughly. "That's enough," he said. "I know quite well what you really think of me. Go indoors. I can see for myself what wants doing." Bridget turned away, not liking to disobey him, and he went on hammering away all round the walls. Then he climbed up onto the roof and mended some holes there, till he had used up all the nails he had brought with him. By this time it was growing dark, and he

The people of the high Alpine valleys were largely self-sufficient. The women spun yarn out of flax, wool, and hemp, which they wove into cloth. Traveling craftsmen would then make many of the clothes and linen goods each household needed, in return receiving food, board, and perhaps money, but more often bartered items.

65

took the sledge out of the goat stall where he had left it, just as Heidi came to find him. He wrapped her up and carried her as he had done the evening before, though he had also to drag the sledge behind him. He knew it would not be safe for her to ride up on it without him beside her, for the wind would soon have blown the coverings away and she would have been

The work of a woodcutter followed several stages. First the tree was felled with an ax or a long two-man saw. Then the bark was peeled off and the log was cut into lengths. Finally it was split into smaller logs that could be neatly stacked until needed.

frozen. So he pulled it after him with one hand, holding Heidi safe and warm in the other arm.

So the winter went on. Poor, blind Grannie was happy again after many sad, dark years, for now she always had something pleasant to look forward to. Every day she listened for Heidi's light step and when the door opened and the little girl came in, she always said, "Praise be, here she is again." Then Heidi would sit down and chatter merrily away. These hours passed so quickly that Grannie never once had to ask Bridget, "Isn't the day nearly over?" Instead, after Heidi had left, she often remarked, "Wasn't that a short afternoon?" and Bridget would agree that it seemed no time since she had cleared away after dinner.

"God keep the child safe and Uncle Alp in a good humor," was the old woman's constant prayer. She often asked Bridget if the child looked well. To that Bridget was always able to reply, "She looks like a rosy apple."

Heidi grew very fond of Peter's Grannie, and when she understood that no one could make her see again, she was very sad. But as Grannie told her over and over again that she didn't mind being blind nearly so much when Heidi was with her, she came down on

Shown above are some examples of a plane, a carpenter's tool that is used to smooth wood or make moldings. The cutting blade shaves the wood in the direction of the fibers to give the surface a perfectly even finish. The planes used for moldings have a variety of names, including hollow plane, round plane, and plough. The trying plane in the center is a long plane used both for "truing up" large work and smoothing it.

the sledge with her grandfather every fine day. He always brought his hammer and nails and any other materials needed, and gradually he repaired the whole cottage, so that Grannie was no longer frightened by noises at night.

This small dairy is equipped to make cheeses for individual households. The cheese maker is pouring milk into a container resting on his large cauldron. In the back of the room are some milking pails, aprons, and other useful items. Some village dairies were cooperatives, in which the people who brought milk would take turns helping the cheese maker to operate the dairy and make the butter and cheese. The cheese maker kept for himself a certain proportion of the cheeses that were made during the course of the day.

5

TWO UNEXPECTED VISITORS

66 She knew how to
handle the goats, and
Daisy and Dusky ran
after her like pet dogs,
bleating with pleasure at
the sound of her
voice. 99

A winter passed and then another happy summer, and
Heidi's second winter on the mountain was nearly over.
She began to look forward eagerly to the spring, when
warm winds would melt the snow and all the blue and
yellow flowers would bloom again. Then she would go
up to the pasture once more, and that she always
enjoyed more than anything. She was now seven and had

According to classical legend, Hyacinthus was a young man renowned for his beauty. When he died, the god Apollo decided to preserve his memory by turning his spilled blood into a flower with petals that formed the Y in his name.

This isolated chalet in the alpine meadows lies at the foot of a high glacial valley whose sheer walls form a deep amphitheater.

learned a great many useful things from her grandfather. She knew how to handle the goats, and Daisy and Dusky ran after her like pet dogs, bleating with pleasure at the sound of her voice. Twice during the winter Peter had brought up messages from the schoolmaster in Dörfli, to say that Uncle Alp must send the child who was living with him to school. She was quite old enough, and ought in fact to have started the winter before. Both times Uncle Alp replied that if the schoolmaster had anything to say to him, he could always be found at home—but he did not mean to send the child to school. These messages Peter delivered faithfully.

When the March sun began to melt the snow on the slopes, the first snowdrops came out. The trees had shaken off their burden of snow and their branches were swaying freely in the wind. Heidi spent her time between the hut, the goat stall, and the fir trees, and kept running to report to her grandfather how much bigger the patch of green grass had grown. One morning, just as she was dashing out of the hut for about the tenth time, she saw an old man standing on the threshold, dressed in black and looking very solemn. He saw she was startled and said in a friendly voice, "You needn't be afraid of me. I'm fond of children.

Come and shake hands. I'm sure you must be Heidi. Where's your grandfather?"

"He's indoors, making wooden spoons," she told him, and showed him in.

He was the old pastor from Dörfli who had been a neighbor of Uncle Alp's when he lived there. "Good morning, my friend," he said, as he went up to him.

Uncle Alp looked up in surprise, and got to his feet. "Good morning, pastor," he replied. Then he pulled forward a chair, adding, "If you don't mind a hard seat, take this one."

"I haven't seen you for a long time," said the pastor, when he had sat down.

"Nor I you," was the reply.

"And now I've come to talk to you about something. I expect you can guess what." He paused and glanced at Heidi who was standing by the door, looking at him with interest.

"Run and take some salt to the goats, Heidi, and stay with them until I fetch you," said her grandfather, and she did as she was told at once.

"That child should have gone to school this winter, if not last," the pastor went on. "The teacher sent you a warning, but you didn't take any notice. What do you intend to do with her, neighbor?"

"I don't intend to send her to school."

66 He was the old pastor from Dörfli who had been a neighbor of Uncle Alp's when he lived there. *99*

This Swiss chalet, jutting out over a lake, is constructed entirely of wood. The living quarters are elevated and surrounded by balconies. The roof, which is covered with wide wooden boards, is stabilized with large rocks.

The pastor stared at Uncle Alp, who was sitting with his arms folded and a very stubborn expression on his face.

"Then what will become of her?" he asked.

"She'll grow up with the goats and the birds. They won't teach her any bad ideas, and she'll be very happy."

"She's not a goat, nor a bird, but a little girl. She may not learn anything bad from such companions, but they won't teach her to read or to write, and it's high time she began. I've come to tell you this in all friendliness, so that you can think it over during the summer and make your plans accordingly. This is the last winter when the child can stay up here without any education. Next winter she must come regularly to school."

"She'll do no such thing," said the old man obstinately.

"Do you really mean that nothing we can say will make you see reason about this? You've been about the world and must have seen and learned a great deal. I should have credited you with more sense, neighbor."

"Would you indeed," said Uncle Alp drily, but his voice showed that he was not quite easy in his mind. "Do you think I'm going to send a little girl like Heidi down the mountain every day next winter, no matter how cold or stormy it may be? And have her come back at night when it is often blowing and snowing so hard that it's difficult for a grown man to keep his feet? Perhaps you remember the queer spells her mother used to have. Such a strain might well make this child devel-op something of the same sort. If anyone tries to force me to send her, I'm quite prepared to go to law about it. Then we'll see what will happen."

"You're right so far," agreed the pastor amiably. "It wouldn't be possible to send her to school from here. And you're fond of her, I can see. Won't you, for her sake, do what you should have done long ago—come back to Dörfli to live? What sort of a life do you lead up here, at odds with God and man? And there's not a soul to help you if you were in any trouble. I can't imagine how even you survive the cold in winter, and I'm amazed that the child can stand up to it at all."

"The child has young blood and a warm bed, I'd have you know," Uncle Alp replied. "And I can always find plenty of wood. My shed is full of it and the fire never goes out the whole winter through. I've no intention of coming back to Dörfli to live. The people there despise me and I them, so it's better for us to keep apart."

"It is not good for you," said the pastor. "I know what you are missing. Believe me, people don't feel so unkindly

In the village of Spulgen, the houses were built along a mountain torrent at a divide in the road, with one branch leading to Lake Maggiore and the other to Lake Como. Three mills and a sawmill were driven by water-power from the river.

toward you as you think. Make your peace with God, neighbor, and ask His forgiveness, where you know you need it. Then come back to Dörfli, and see how differently people will receive you, and how happy you can become again."

He stood up and held out his hand. "I shall count on seeing you back among us next winter, old friend," he said. "I should be sorry if we had to put any pressure upon you. Give me your hand and promise you'll come down and live among us again and be reconciled to God and to your neighbors."

Uncle Alp shook hands with him, but said slowly, "I know you mean well, but I can't do what you ask. That's final. I shan't send the child to school, nor come back to the village to live."

"May God help you, then," said the pastor and he went sadly out of the hut and down the mountain.

He left Uncle Alp out of humor. After dinner when Heidi said as usual, "Now it's time to go to Grannie's," he only replied, "Not today," and didn't say another word that day. Next morning she asked again if they were going to Grannie's, and he only said gruffly, "We'll see." But before the dinner dishes had been cleared away they had another visitor. This time it was Detie. She was wearing a smart hat with a feather and a long dress which swept the ground as she walked—and the floor of the hut was not particularly good for it. Uncle Alp looked her up and down in silence. However Detie was all amiability, and started to talk at once.

"How well Heidi looks," she exclaimed. "I hardly recognize her! You've certainly looked after her all right.

These two men, a priest and a hiker carrying a rucksack, are following a mule track. The path is steep and rocky, barely wide enough for a loaded mule to pass.

Of course I always intended to come back for her because I know she must be in your way, but two years ago I just didn't know what else to do with her. I've been on the lookout for a good home for her ever since, and that's why I'm here now. I've heard of a wonderful chance for her. I've been into it all thoroughly and everything's all right. It's a chance in a million! The family I work for have got some very rich relations who live in one of the best houses in Frankfurt. They've a little girl who's paralyzed on one side and very delicate. She has to be in a wheelchair all the time and has lessons by herself with a tutor. That's terribly dull for her and she longs for a little playmate. They've been talking about it at my place because of course my family, being relations, are very sorry for her and would like to help her. That's how I heard what they wanted—a simple, unspoiled child to come and stay with her, they said, someone a bit out of the ordinary. I thought of Heidi at once, and I went and saw the lady who keeps house for them. I told her all about Heidi and she said she thought she would do. Isn't that wonderful? Isn't Heidi a lucky girl? And, if they like her, and anything were to happen to their daughter, which is quite likely, you know, it might well be that . . ."

"Have you nearly finished?" Uncle Alp interrupted her, having listened so far in silence.

Among the privileged classes, children often received their education from a governess who lived with the family. Here, a governess looks after her ailing charge.

This church, which sits at the bottom of a small valley, has a particularly high and graceful steeple, which is clearly visible from a distance.

Detie tossed her head in exasperation. "Anyone would think I'd been telling you something quite unimportant," she said. "There's no one else in the whole district who wouldn't be thankful to hear such a piece of news."

"Tell them then," he said drily, "it doesn't interest me."

Detie flew up like a rocket at these words. "If that's what you think, let me tell you something more. The child will soon be eight and she doesn't know a thing and you won't let her learn. Oh yes, they told me in Dörfli about your not sending her to school or to church. But she's my sister's child and I'm still responsible for her welfare. And when the chance of such good fortune has come her way, only a person who doesn't care what happens to anyone could want to keep her from it. But I shan't let you, I warn you, and everyone in Dörfli's on my side. Also I'd advise you to think twice before taking the matter to court. You might find things being remembered which you'd rather forget. There's no knowing what may come to light in a court of law."

"That's enough," thundered the old man, with his eyes ablaze. "Take her then and spoil her. But don't ever bring her back to me. I don't want to see her with a feather in her hat or hear her talk as you have done today." And he strode out of the hut.

"You've made Grandfather angry," said Heidi, giving her aunt a far-from-friendly look.

"He'll get over it," said Detie. "Come on now, where are your clothes?"

"I'm not coming," said Heidi.

"Don't talk nonsense," snapped her aunt, but continued in a coaxing tone, "you don't know what a good time you're going to have." She went to the cupboard and took out Heidi's things and made them into a bundle. "Put your hat on. It's pretty shabby, but it'll have to do. Hurry now, we must be off."

"I'm not coming," Heidi repeated.

"Don't be stupid and obstinate like one of those old goats!" snapped Detie again. "I suppose it's from them you've learned such behavior. Just you try to understand now. You saw how angry your grandfather was. You heard him say he didn't want to see us again. He *wants* you to go with me, so you'd better obey if you don't want to make him angrier still. Besides you can't think how nice it is in Frankfurt and how much there is going on there. And if you don't like it you can always come back here. Grandfather will be in a better mood by then."

"Could I come straight back again this evening?" asked Heidi.

"Well, no. We shall only get as far as Mayenfeld today. Tomorrow we'll go on by train, but you can always get back the same way if you want to come home. It doesn't take long." Detie caught hold of Heidi with one hand, and tucked the bundle of clothes under the other arm, and so they set off down the mountain.

It was still too early in the year for Peter to be taking the goats up to the pasture, so he was at school in

This nineteenth-century poster for the Swiss railways announces the new rail link between Lucerne and Engelberg. Bringing railway lines into the mountains called for great technical prowess. The track had to follow the gentlest slope possible, which meant that cuts, fills, and embankments were needed; there were bridges, overpasses, and tunnels to be built; the superstructure was then put in place, consisting of the ballast, rails, ties, switches, and crossings; and there were still the signals to install before the rolling stock (the locomotive and cars) could be brought onto the new rails.

66 'Tomorrow we'll go on by train, but you can always get back the same way if you want to come.' 99

Dörfli—or should have been. But every now and then he played truant, for he thought school a great waste of time and could see no point in trying to learn to read. He liked much better to wander off and gather wood, which was always needed. On this particular day he was just coming home with an enormous bundle of hazel twigs when he saw Heidi and Detie. "Where are you going?" he asked, as they came up to him.

"I'm going to Frankfurt on a visit with Auntie," said Heidi, "but I'll come in and see Grannie first. She'll be expecting me."

"No, you won't, there's no time for that," said Detie firmly, as Heidi tried to pull her hand away. "You can go and see her when you come back." And she kept tight hold of her and hurried on. She was afraid Heidi would change her mind again, if she went in there, and the old woman would certainly take her side. Peter rushed into the cottage and flung his sticks on the table as hard as he could. He just had to relieve his feelings somehow. Grannie jumped up in alarm and cried, "Whatever's that noise?" His mother, who had almost been knocked out of her chair, said in her usual patient voice, "What's the matter, Peterkin? Why are you so wild?"

"She's taking Heidi away," he shouted.

"Who is? Where are they going?" asked Grannie anxiously, though she could guess the answer, for her daughter had seen Detie pass on her way up to Uncle Alp's, and had told her about it then. Now she opened the window and called beseechingly, "Don't take the child away from us, Detie!" But they had hurried on, and though they heard her voice, they couldn't make out the words, but Detie guessed what they were and pulled Heidi along as fast as she could go.

This man is wearing a wooden carrying frame with two levels. It allows him to transport heavy loads on his back, especially bundles of wood. This kind of carrier is very useful in the mountains, where the slope forces a walker to bend forward and lean on his or her walking stick.

"That was Grannie calling. I want to go and see her," said Heidi, trying again to free her hand.

"We can't stop for that, we're late as it is," retorted Detie. "We don't want to miss the train. Just you think of the wonderful time you'll have in Frankfurt, and when you come back again—if indeed you ever want to, once you're there—you can bring a present for Grannie."

"Can I really?" Heidi asked, pleased with this idea. "What could I get for her?"

"Something nice to eat perhaps. I

expect she'd like the soft white rolls they have in town. She must find black bread almost too hard to eat now."

"Yes, she does. I've seen her give her piece to Peter because she couldn't bite it. Let's hurry Detie. Can we get to Frankfurt today? Then I could come back at once with the rolls." She started to run so fast that Detie, hampered by the bundle of clothes under her arm, found it hard work to keep up with her. But she was glad to get along so quickly because they were coming to Dörfli where she knew people would start asking questions in a way which might upset the child again.

Sure enough as they went through the village, remarks came from all sides. "Is she running away from Uncle Alp?" "Fancy, she's still alive!"

"She looks well enough." To all questions Detie replied, "I can't stop to talk. You can see we're in a great hurry and we've a long way to go." She was thankful when they had left the village behind. Heidi didn't say another word, but ran on as quickly as she could.

66 Detie caught hold of Heidi with one hand and they set off down the mountain. **99**

From that day Uncle Alp grew more silent and forbidding than ever. On the rare occasions when he passed through Dörfli with his basket of cheeses on his back and a heavy stick in his hand, mothers kept their children well out of the way, for he looked so wild. He never spoke to anyone, but went on down to the valley, where he sold his wares and bought bread and meat with the proceeds. People used to gather in little groups after he had passed, gossiping about his strange looks and behavior. They all agreed it was a mercy that the child had escaped from him and reminded one another how fast she had been running down the mountain, as if she had been afraid he was coming after them to fetch her back.

But Peter's Grannie always stood up for him. Whenever anyone came to bring her wool to spin or to fetch the finished work, she took care to mention how well he had looked after the child and how kind he had been about repairing their cottage, which might otherwise have fallen down by this time. The villagers found this hard to believe and decided that the old woman did not know what she was talking about, being blind and probably rather deaf as well.

Uncle Alp never went near her cottage again, but he had done his work well and it was now strong enough to

The decoration on these houses from the north of Switzerland shows a perfect mastery of woodworking: the balustrade is fretted, the pillars and crosspieces carved; even the ends of the beams are decoratively finished and the door frames wonderfully sculpted. The abundance and delicacy of the designs gives the whole an airy feeling, as though the huge structures were built of wooden lacework.

stand up to the stormy weather. Without Heidi's visits, Grannie found the days long and empty and she grew very sad and often used to say, "I should like to hear that dear child's voice just once again before I die."

Stagecoaches often stopped in front of the post office, for these public, horse-drawn carriages carried the mail as well as passengers. Baggage was loaded onto the roof under a tarpaulin. The passengers rode inside while the driver sat on the box seat in front.

66 'Sometimes he puts
the book right up to his
face, as though he were
dreadfully short-sighted,
but I know he's only
yawning behind it.'99

Frankfurt was formerly a
somewhat politically
independent town
governed by an assembly
of wealthy aristocrats.
Splendid gabled houses
still remain from that
period.

6

A NEW LIFE BEGINS

The house in Frankfurt to which Heidi was being taken
belonged to a wealthy man called Mr. Sesemann. His
only daughter, Clara, was an invalid and spent all her
days in a wheelchair, in which she was pushed wherever
she wanted to go. She was a very patient child, with a
thin, pale face and mild, blue eyes. Her mother had been
dead for a long time, and since then her father had
employed as housekeeper a worthy but very disagreeable
person called Miss Rottenmeier. She looked after Clara
and was in charge of all the servants. As Mr. Sesemann
was often away from home on business, he left all the

household affairs in her hands, on the sole condition that Clara was never to be crossed in any way.

On the evening when Heidi was expected, Clara was sitting, as she usually did, in a pleasant, comfortable room, next to the big dining room. It was called the study because of the big, glass-fronted bookcase which stood against one wall, and it was here that Clara did her lessons. Now she kept looking at the big clock on the wall, which she felt must be going more slowly than usual, and finally, in a tone of impatience which was rare with her, she asked, "Isn't it nearly time, Miss Rottenmeier?"

That lady was sitting very stiff and straight at a small work table, sewing. She wore a jacket with a high

When Heidi went to live in Frankfurt, in the 1880s, the new German Empire or "Reich" had been in existence for about ten years. It covered a much greater area than Germany does today. The empire was formed at Versailles in 1870 to mark the defeat of France and the triumph of Prussia, whose chancellor, Prince Otto von Bismarck (1815–1889), managed to unite all the independent states of Germany under Prussian leadership. Alsace and a part of Lorraine were conquered from France during the war and now belonged to the new German Empire. At right is a mid-nineteenth-century view of the German Empire. Frankfurt, which became a part of Prussia in 1866, developed into a great center for industry, trade, and banking, a position that it retains today. The Main River, a tributary of the Rhine, flows through Frankfurt; the metal bridge and steam-powered paddle-wheeler in the picture above attest to the city's rise, and stand in contrast to the old half-timbered buildings from earlier periods.

collar and had a sort of turban on her head, which made her look very imposing.

"Shouldn't they be here by now?" repeated Clara, still more impatiently.

At that very moment Detie was standing with Heidi at the front door. The coachman, whose name was John, had just brought round the carriage so she asked him whether it would be convenient for her to see Miss Rottenmeier.

"That's not my business," he replied. "You'd better ring for Sebastian."

Detie did so and presently a manservant came hurrying downstairs. He wore a smart coat with big round buttons, and his eyes were as round and big as the buttons.

"Is it convenient, please, for me to see Miss Rottenmeier?" asked Detie.

"That's not my job," said Sebastian, "ring that other bell for Tinette," and he went away.

Detie rang again and this time a smart maid appeared, with a snowy white cap on her head and a very pert look on her face.

"What do you want?" she called saucily from the top of the stairs.

Detie repeated her question, and the maid went away but soon came back to say, "You are expected." So Heidi and Detie went up and followed Tinette to the study, where they stood respectfully just inside the door. Detie kept tight hold of Heidi, not being quite certain how she might behave in these strange surroundings. Miss Rottenmeier got up slowly and came over to

The bicycle was developed at the end of the nineteenth century, as were rubber tires and spring suspension, which both improved the comfort of wheeled transport. At the same time, advances in technology and industrialization made it possible to build vehicles for the handicapped, such as the wheelchairs pictured here. They remained very expensive, however, and with no social-services system to distribute them, they were available only to the most privileged, such as the Sesemann family in *Heidi*.

Middle-class families kept servants, and the number of servants a household had indicated its social standing. Domestic work was frequently taken by country people wanting to come to the city, and was often provided to them through a placement office. The arrogance and suspicion these "house servants" were often subject to is clear from the 1889 engraving above, where a notice warns that one should keep a close eye on one's wallet! *Below*, a country girl has presented a letter of recommendation to a potential mistress interviewing her.

inspect the companion who had been proposed for the daughter of the house. She did not appear to like what she saw, for Heidi was wearing a shabby cotton frock and a shapeless old hat, and was staring up with undisguised astonishment at the extraordinary headdress the lady wore.

"What's your name?" asked Miss Rottenmeier, after staring hard at her for some moments. Heidi told her in a nice clear voice.

"That can't be your proper name, surely? What were you christened?"

"I don't remember," said Heidi.

"That's no way to answer. Is the child half-witted or impertinent?" Miss Rottenmeier said to Detie.

"If you please, Ma'am, I'll speak for her. She's not used to strangers," Detie replied, giving Heidi a little push as punishment for her unsuitable reply. "She's not half-witted I can assure you, nor impertinent either, but she doesn't know any better. She says the first thing that comes into her head. She's never been in a house like this before and no one's taught her how to behave. But she's bright and quick to learn if anyone would take a little trouble with her. So please excuse her, Ma'am. She was christened Adelheid after her mother, my dead sister."

"Well, at least that is a reasonable name, but the

child seems to me very young. I told you we wanted someone of Miss Clara's own age, so that they could do lessons together and be real companions. Miss Clara is twelve. How old is this child?"

Detie had expected this question and was prepared with an answer. "To tell you the truth, Ma'am," she said glibly, "I can't remember just how old she is, but about ten I think."

"I'll soon be eight," said Heidi. "Grandfather told me so."

Detie gave her another cross little push, but Heidi was quite unaware of having said anything wrong.

"Not yet eight!" exclaimed Miss Rottenmeier. "That's at least four years too young. What's the good of bringing her here?" She turned to Heidi and went on, "What books have you been using in your lessons?"

"None," said Heidi.

"What's that you say? How did you learn to read then?"

"I haven't learned to read," Heidi replied. "Nor has Peter."

"Good gracious me, can't read at your age!" cried Miss Rottenmeier in dismay. "Impossible! What have you learned then?"

"Nothing," said Heidi frankly.

There was a strained silence, while Miss Rotten-meier grasped the situation. "Really, Detie," she said at last, "I don't know what you were thinking about to bring that child here. She won't do at all."

But Detie was not going to give in easily, and replied with spirit, "If you please, I thought she would be just

Schools had existed in German towns and villages for a long time, but education was not mandatory and was often fairly primitive. Schools were sometimes in session only during the winter, when there was no work to be done in the fields. Students of all ages were mixed in together, with the elder helping to give instruction to the younger. Corporal punishment was the norm, as the schoolmaster's cane would suggest. The teacher often received only bartered goods as payment, along with various gifts of food, drink, and firewood. He was sometimes caricatured in the writing of the period as a brutal drunkard, or as a hapless fellow who was also called on to fill in as the church sexton, organist, choir-master, and secretary. Under Chancellor Bismarck, however, public education steadily improved.

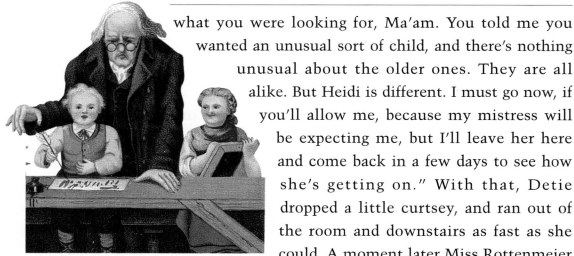

what you were looking for, Ma'am. You told me you wanted an unusual sort of child, and there's nothing unusual about the older ones. They are all alike. But Heidi is different. I must go now, if you'll allow me, because my mistress will be expecting me, but I'll leave her here and come back in a few days to see how she's getting on." With that, Detie dropped a little curtsey, and ran out of the room and downstairs as fast as she could. A moment later Miss Rottenmeier went after her, for there were many things to be discussed if the child was to stay, and apparently Detie was determined to leave her there.

For the wealthy, who preferred to keep their children apart from the children of the poor, it was common to employ a tutor or private schoolmaster, particularly for the elementary-school years. Later the children would go on to secondary school, or "gymnasium," which at the time was almost wholly reserved for the children of the middle class, and was a place where one began to forge the social bonds that would be useful later in life; afterward came university. At the time of Bismarck, the fashion for private tutoring was on the wane, but it still persisted in the cities. Many of the great German writers of the nineteenth-century who came from humble backgrounds worked as tutors to wealthy families. The children shown above are writing with a goose-quill pen, whereas the Industrial Revolution would soon make it possible to use metal-nibbed pens, which were stronger and needed no sharpening.

All this time Heidi had not moved, not even when Detie left her. Clara, who had watched everything in silence from her wheelchair, now called her over.

"Do you want to be called Heidi or Adelheid?" she asked.

"Everyone calls me Heidi, that's my name," the little girl replied.

"Well, I'll call you that too. It's a queer name, but it suits you. I've never seen anyone quite like you before. Have you always had short, curly hair?"

"Yes, I think so," replied Heidi cheerfully.

"Are you glad you've come here?" continued Clara.

"No, but I shall be going home again tomorrow, with some nice rolls for Grannie."

"You are a funny child. As a matter of fact, you've been brought to Frankfurt expressly to keep me company and have lessons with me. We might have some fun too, as you can't even read. Lessons are often very dull. Mr. Usher, that's my tutor, comes every day from ten to two, and it's such a long time. Sometimes he puts the book right up to his face, as though he were dreadfully short-sighted, but I know he's only yawning behind it. Then Miss Rottenmeier takes out a handkerchief and holds it up to her face, as though she were crying, but really she's yawning too. That makes me want to yawn, and I have to stifle it because if I yawned she'd be sure to say I must be feeling poorly, and I'd have to take a dose of cod-liver oil, which is the most horrible stuff imaginable. But now I shall be able to listen while you learn to read, and that'll be much more amusing."

Heidi shook her head doubtfully.

"But of course you will learn to read—everyone has to," Clara went on quickly. "And Mr. Usher is very kind. He never gets cross and he'll explain everything to you. You probably won't understand what he's talking about at first, but don't ever say so, or he'll go on and on forever, and you still won't understand any better. Later on, when you've learned a little, I expect you'll see what he means all right."

Miss Rottenmeier came back at this point. She had not been quick enough to catch Detie, and was very much put out, for she did not see how to get out of this awkward situation, for which she was really responsible as she had certainly agreed to Heidi's being fetched. She walked about restlessly between the study and the dining room, and presently came upon Sebastian who had just finished setting the table and was looking it over to make sure he had not forgotten anything.

The advertisement below promotes a "miracle" cod-liver oil whose smell is so pleasant that the little blond girl has apparently forgotten how nauseating it tastes. Rich in vitamin D, cod-liver oil was an excellent remedy for rickets and the various illnesses suffered by the children of that period, many of whom lived in cities polluted by coal smoke and infested with diseases such as tuberculosis and diphtheria, against which doctors were helpless. Being given cod-liver oil was a child's great fear: the boy in black in the lower picture is putting up a good struggle. The oil was traditionally produced in Norway by pressing the livers of freshly caught cod.

When the cat is away, the mice will play. Here, these servants are taking advantage of their masters' absence to ape their manners and help themselves to their food and drink. Perhaps they are avenging themselves for the slights they receive on a daily basis.

Below is a teapot with a small attached warmer, an item produced for the affluent middle class of that era.

"Finish your thinking some other time and see about serving the meal," she snapped, and then called, in a peremptory tone, for Tinette, who minced into the room with a very high and mighty expression on her face which made even Miss Rottenmeier swallow her anger, and she said as coolly as she could, "See that the room is prepared for the girl who has just come. Everything has been put ready, but it wants dusting."

"Oh certainly," retorted Tinette impudently, as she flounced out of the room.

Sebastian too was furious, but had not dared to answer back. He showed it by banging open the double doors leading from the dining room to the study. Then he slouched over to wheel Clara in to supper, and as he paused to manipulate the handle of the chair, he saw Heidi staring at him. This annoyed him still more, and he growled, "Well, what are you staring at?"

"You look like Peter the goat boy," she replied. Miss Rottenmeier came back into the study just then, and held up her hands in disgust.

"What a way to talk to the servants!" she exclaimed. "She simply hasn't an idea how to behave."

Clara was wheeled up to the table, and Sebastian lifted her onto an armchair. Miss Rottenmeier sat beside her and motioned to Heidi to take the seat opposite. It was a big table just for the three of them and left plenty of room for Sebastian to stand beside each, as he handed the dishes. Beside Heidi's plate lay a nice white roll, and her eyes lit up at sight of it. She did not take it, however, until Sebastian was offering her the dish of baked fish, then feeling she must be able to trust anyone who looked so like Peter, she said to him, "May I have this?" and pointed to the roll.

This household scale was used to measure ingredients for the precisely calibrated recipes of middle-class cooking, as opposed to the cooking of the poor, which was often very primitive. It also made it possible to verify whether the servants who did the shopping were honest.

Sebastian nodded and looked out of the corner of his eye to see how Miss Rottenmeier was taking it. When Heidi took up the roll and put it in her pocket, he hardly knew how to keep his face straight, but it would have been more than his place was worth to show amusement. He was not supposed to speak or to move until she had helped herself from the dish, so he continued to stand silently beside her, waiting. At length she looked up at him and said in a tone of surprise, "Am I to have some of that too?"

He nodded again, making a very odd face in his efforts to stifle his laughter.

"Give me some then," said Heidi, looking down at her plate.

"You can put the dish on the table and come back later," said the stern voice of Miss Rottenmeier, and Sebastian made for the door immediately.

"I see I shall have to begin right at the beginning with you, Adelheid," that lady continued with a pained blink of the eyes. "Now, this is how you should help yourself at table," and she proceeded to show how it should be done. "And understand, you must never speak to Sebastian during a meal, except to give him an order or to ask for something. And you must never speak to any of the servants in that familiar way. You'll address me as Ma'am, as you'll hear everyone else do. As for Clara, it's for her to say what you are to call her."

"Clara, of course," put in the invalid.

Miss Rottenmeier then held forth on how Heidi was to behave at every moment of the day, issuing instructions about getting up in the morning, and going to bed at night, about going out and coming in, about shutting doors, and keeping things tidy, and so on and on. In the middle of it all Heidi suddenly dropped off to sleep, for she had been up since five o'clock and traveling all day.

At last Miss Rottenmeier came to the end of her lecture, and said, "Now, Adelheid, do you understand what I've been saying?"

"Heidi's asleep," Clara remarked with a smile. It was a long time since she had known a meal pass so agreeably.

66 In the middle of it all Heidi suddenly dropped off to sleep, for she had been up since five o'clock and traveling all day. **99**

"That child's behavior is really incredible," exclaimed Miss Rottenmeier, much annoyed, and she rang the bell so violently that Sebastian and Tinette both came hurrying in, nearly knocking each other over. But the commotion did not wake Heidi, and it was quite difficult to rouse her sufficiently to take her to bed.

The room which had been prepared for her was at the other end of the house and, to get to it, she had to go past the study, and past Clara's bedroom and Miss Rottenmeier's sitting room.

7

A BAD DAY FOR ROTTENMEIER

❝ Heidi awoke next morning and looked around her, quite forgetting all that had happened to her the day before. She couldn't think where she was.**❞**

Heidi awoke next morning and looked around her, quite forgetting all that had happened to her the day before. She couldn't think where she was. She rubbed her eyes and looked again, but that made no difference. She was in a big room, in a high white bed. There were long white curtains in front of the windows and two big arm-chairs and a sofa, covered with some beautiful flowery material; there was a round table, and on a washstand in the corner stood a number of things that she had never seen before. All at once she remembered all that had happened to her overnight, particularly the instructions the tall lady had given her, so far, that is, as she had heard them.

A view of the old city of Frankfurt. This square, which still exists today, is the center and the symbol of the town. The three structures with stepped gables date back to the Middle Ages, and once formed the city hall, called the *Römer*. On the second floor of the central building was the great room where banquets were held in honor of the newly elected emperors of the Holy Roman Empire, whose coronations were held at the Frankfurt cathedral. In the foreground are two horse-drawn carriages known as barouches, which were the taxis of the day, and a gas lamp such as was used when Heidi lived there.

She jumped out of bed and dressed quickly. Then she went first to one window, then to the other, and tried to pull back the curtains so that she could see what was outside. They were too heavy to pull so she crept behind them, but then the windows were so high that she could only just peep through them. And wherever she looked there was nothing to be seen but walls and windows. She began to feel rather frightened. At Grandfather's she had always gone out of doors first thing in the morning to have a good look round, to see whether the sky was blue and the sun shining, and to say good morning to the trees and flowers. She ran from window to window frantically, trying to open them, like a wild bird in a cage, seeking a way through the bars to freedom. She felt sure that if she could see what was outside, she would find grass somewhere, green grass with the last snow just melting from it. But though she pushed and tugged and tried to put her little fingers under the frames, the windows stayed tight shut. After a while she gave up. "Perhaps if I went out of doors and round to the back of the house, I'd find some grass," she thought. "I know there were only stones in front."

Just then there was a tap at the door and Tinette put her head round it, snapped out, "Breakfast's ready," and shut it again quickly. Heidi hadn't the least idea what she meant, but she had sounded so fierce that Heidi thought she was being told to stay where she was. She found a little stool under the table and sat down, to see what would happen next. It was not long before Miss Rottenmeier came bustling in, very annoyed, and scolding all the time. "What's the matter with you, Adelheid? Don't you even know what breakfast is? Come along at once." This at least Heidi could understand, and she followed her obediently into the dining room. Clara had been waiting there for some time but gave her a friendly greeting. She looked more cheerful than usual, for she had an idea she was going to have quite an interesting day.

Little is left of the historic old city of Frankfurt, which was heavily bombed in World War II. Johann Wolfgang von Goethe (1749–1832), one of Germany's most famous writers, grew up there. Perhaps he played in these narrow little streets, which today no longer exist.

Breakfast passed without further incident. Heidi ate her bread and butter quite nicely, and when the meal was over Clara was wheeled into the study and Heidi was sent with her and told to wait there until Mr. Usher arrived. As soon as the two girls were alone, Heidi asked, "How can I look out of the window and see what's down below?"

"First the window has to be opened," said Clara, with a smile.

"But they won't open," Heidi answered.

"Oh yes, they will, but you can't do it yourself and nor can I. But Sebastian will open one for you if you ask him."

Heidi was relieved to hear that. Then Clara began to ask about her life at home and Heidi was soon chattering away merrily about the mountains and the goats and all

In Heidi's time, just as today, children who were learning to read had to start by recognizing the letters of the alphabet. Illustrated books, called abecedariums, were used. *Top*: the letter combinations *ie-ck-tz* (which are in the words *Biene-Krücke-Katze*, meaning "bee, crutch, cat") are illustrated. Until World War II, most German texts were printed using characters that came down from the Middle Ages and were very difficult to read. This was known as Gothic lettering, because of the Goths, a German people, and because of the period during medieval times when this particular alphabet was used. The image above shows a swan (*Schwan*) to illustrate the letter combination *sch*.

the other things she loved so well.

While they talked the tutor arrived, but instead of coming straight to the study as usual, he was waylaid by Miss Rottenmeier who took him into the dining room to explain the awkward situation in which she found herself.

"Some time ago when Mr. Sesemann was in Paris on business," she began, "I wrote to tell him that Clara ought to have a companion of her own age. She wanted it, and so did I, for I thought she might work harder at her lessons if she had some competition, and also the companionship would be pleasant and good for her. It would also spare me the necessity to keep her amused all the time, which, believe me, is not easy. Her father agreed, but insisted that the other child should be treated exactly the same as his own daughter. He wrote he would not have any child in his house put upon in any way. A most uncalled-for remark, I must say. No one here would be likely to do any such thing!"

She then told him of Heidi's arrival and how utterly unsuitable she found her, in every way. "Fancy, she doesn't even know her alphabet, and has no idea how to behave in polite society. There seems to me only one way out of this dreadful situation, and that is for you to say that it is impossible to teach these two children together without holding back Clara quite disastrously. That would surely be reason enough to persuade Mr. Sesemann to send this Swiss girl home again."

Mr. Usher was a cautious man, who always tried to look at both sides of any problem, so after several politely consoling remarks, he went on to say that perhaps things might not be as bad as she feared. If the child was backward in some ways, she might be ahead in others, and with regular lessons it might be possible to bring her on quite quickly. Miss Rottenmeier saw that she was not likely to get the support she wanted from this quarter, for obviously the tutor did not at all mind teaching Heidi her ABC from the very beginning. She showed him to the study door, therefore, and watched him go inside, but the thought of having to watch Heidi at her letters was more than she could bear. She walked about the dining room restlessly, wondering how the servants had better address Adelheid, for Mr. Sesemann's instruction that the child was to be treated just like his daughter could only refer to them, she thought. She was not left for long with her thoughts, however. Suddenly there was a tremendous clatter in the study, as though a lot of things had fallen down, and she heard someone call for Sebastian. She hurried into the room and found the floor strewn with books, writing paper, an inkwell, and the tablecloth, from under which a stream of ink was flowing. Heidi was nowhere to be seen.

"This is a fine to-do,"

Below, a representation of an elementary-school class in Germany in 1872. Under Bismarck, education was improved at many levels of society. Prussia, now a great country, needed a vast army of well-trained workers and soldiers. The French philosopher Victor Cousin (1792–1867) sardonically described Germany as "a classic nation of barracks and schoolhouses." Yet in Prussia in 1871 only 12 to 13 percent of the population over ten years of age was illiterate, while illiteracy in France was still at 24 percent and in England at 30 percent.

Pictured here is the driver of a hansom cab, wearing a hard leather hat and waiting for a fare to appear. The money pack at his waist signals that he was not a private coachman, but was equivalent to the taxi drivers of our own day. Exposed all day and all night to the weather, and often sleeping in their carriages, the drivers of hansom cabs had to be physically strong and were known for their coarse and loutish ways. Because a ride in a cab cost more than common people could afford, they usually walked instead; having shoes caked with mud was an infallible sign of low social status.

said Miss Rottenmeier, wringing her hands. "Books, carpet, tablecloth, all covered with ink. Never have I seen such a mess. Of course it's all that wretched child!"

Mr. Usher stood looking about him in dismay. Even he could not find anything consoling to say about what had happened, though Clara seemed greatly amused by it.

"Yes, Heidi did it—quite by accident," she said. "You must not punish her. She just rushed across the room and caught the tablecloth as she went by, and swept everything on to the floor with it. There were a lot of carriages going by in the street and I expect she wanted to look at them. I daresay she has never seen such a thing in her life before."

"What did I tell you, Mr. Usher? The child is quite impossible. She doesn't even understand that she ought to sit still and listen during a lesson. And where has she got to now? I suppose she's run out of the front door. Whatever would Mr. Sesemann say?"

She hurried off downstairs and found Heidi by the open door, looking up and down the street with a puzzled expression.

"What are you thinking of? What do you mean by running away from your lessons like that?" scolded Miss Rottenmeier.

"I heard the fir trees rustling, but I can't see them anywhere. I can't even hear them now," replied Heidi.

It was the passing of light carriage wheels which she had mistaken for the wind blowing through the trees and which had sent her rushing joyfully downstairs to investigate, but the carriages had gone by before she got there.

"Fir trees indeed! Do you think Frankfurt is in the middle of a wood? Just you come with me and see what a mess you've made," and Heidi was led back to the study, where she was most surprised to see what havoc she had wrought in her headlong flight from the room.

"Don't you ever do such a thing again," said Miss Rottenmeier, pointing to the floor. "You must sit still during lessons and pay attention. If you don't, I shall have to tie you to your chair. Is that understood?"

"Yes. I will sit still," replied Heidi, accepting this as another rule that she must obey.

Sebastian and Tinette were sent for to clear up the mess and Mr. Usher bowed and took his leave, saying there would be no more lessons. Certainly no one had been bored that day!

Along the modern streets in Frankfurt, there remain old houses dating back as far as the medieval period. In some of these houses, the side facing the street is gabled and the external walls are half-timbered—that is, framed with wooden timbers and the space between filled in with plaster or a mix of clay and straw. The ornaments, known as finials, that crown the roofs are shaped into decorative symbols. The high attics with their several rows of dormer windows were used to store goods or to dry foodstuffs. The fact that there is an automobile shown indicates that this image dates back to the very end of the nineteenth century, as Daimler-Benz cars were first produced in the 1890s.

Clara always had to rest in the afternoons and Miss Rottenmeier told Heidi she could do as she pleased during that time. So after dinner, when the little invalid had settled down to sleep and the housekeeper had gone to her room, Heidi felt the moment had come to carry out something she had been planning. But she needed help, so she waited in the passage outside the dining room for Sebastian who presently came upstairs from the kitchen with a big tray of silver to be put away in the dining room cupboard. She stepped forward as he reached the last stair and said, "You, there," for she was uncertain how to address him after what Miss Rottenmeier had told her.

"What do you want, Miss?" he asked, rather crossly.

"I only want to ask you something. It's nothing naughty like this morning," she added, for he seemed in rather a bad mood and she thought that might be because of the ink on the carpet.

"All right," he said more pleasantly, "what is it, Miss?"

"My name's not Miss, it's Heidi."

"Miss Rottenmeier told us to call you that," he replied.

"Oh, well, I suppose you must then," she said in a small voice. She was quite aware that that lady's orders had to be obeyed. "And in that case, I

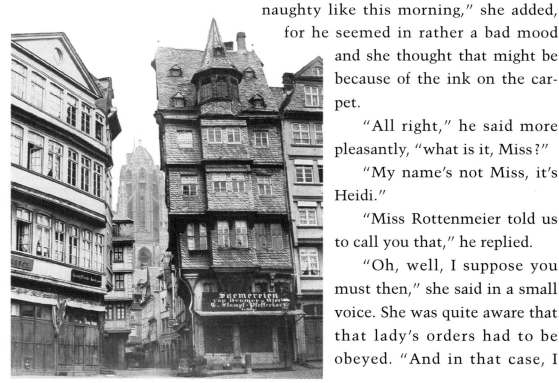

have three names," she added with a sigh.

"What is it you want to ask, Miss?" asked Sebastian, going into the dining room with his tray. Heidi followed.

"Can you open a window, Sebastian?"

"Of course," he said and threw open the big casement. Heidi was too small to see out. Her chin only came up to the sill, but he brought her a high wooden stool and said, "If you climb on that, Miss, you'll be able to see what's down below." She got up on it, but after a quick glance, turned back with a very disappointed face.

"There's nothing but stony streets," she said sadly. "What should I see on the other side of the house, Sebastian?"

"Nothing different."

She could not understand what living in a town meant, nor that the train had carried her so far away from the mountains and pastures.

"Then where can I go to see over the whole valley?"

"You'd have to go somewhere high up, a church tower like that one over there with the gold ball on top," he said, pointing. "You'd see ever so far from there."

Heidi climbed down from the stool and ran downstairs and out of the front door. But she did not find the tower just across the road as it had seemed from the window. She ran right down the street, but couldn't see it anywhere. She turned into a side street and walked on and on. She passed a lot of people, but they all seemed in such a hurry that

66 He brought her a high wooden stool and said, 'If you climb on that, Miss, you'll be able to see what's down below.' 99

101

she did not like to stop one of them to ask the way. Then she saw a boy standing at a corner, with a small hurdy-gurdy on his back and a tortoise in his arms. She went up to him and asked:

"Where's the tower with the gold ball on top?"

"I don't know."

"Who can I ask then?"

"Don't know."

"Do you know any church with a high tower?"

"Yes, one."

"Well, come and show me."

"What will you give me, if I do?" asked the boy, holding out his hand.

She felt in her pocket and brought out a little card with a wreath of red roses painted on it which Clara had given her that morning. She looked at it for a moment, rather regretfully, but decided it was worth sacrificing to see the view over the valley.

"There, would you like this?" she asked, holding it out to him. He shook his head.

"What do you want then?" she asked, glad to put her treasure back in the pocket.

"Money."

"I haven't got any money," said Heidi, "but Clara has and I

As retirement benefits did not exist, many elderly people with no families to support them were obliged to earn a living working in marginal trades, just as this organ grinder is doing. The little girl who stands watching with her governess is fascinated. Hanging from the organ is a sheaf of papers with the words to the songs; these were sold to the audience for a nominal price so that all could join in.

expect she'll give me some for you. How much do you want?"

"Two pennies."

"All right. Now let's go."

They went off together down a long street. "What's that on your back?" asked Heidi.

"It's an organ. When I turn the handle, music comes out. Here we are," he added, for they had reached an old church which had a high tower. The doors were fast shut, however.

"How can I get in?" asked Heidi.

"Don't know."

Then she caught sight of a bell in the wall.

"Do you think I can ring, like they do for Sebastian?" she asked.

"Don't know," he said again.

She went up to the wall and pulled with all her might at the bell.

"Wait for me, if I go up, because I don't know the way home, and you will have to show me."

"What will you give me if I do?"

"What do you want?"

"Another twopence."

Then they heard the old lock being turned from within, the door opened with a creak, and an old man peered out. He looked very annoyed when he saw the children. "What do you mean by bringing me all this way down?" he demanded. "Can't you read what it says under the bell: 'For those who wish to climb the tower'?"

The boy jerked his thumb at Heidi, but said nothing.

Above, a vendor of rattles, which were known as "forest devils" and were thought to keep away wolves and evil spirits, but finally became simply children's noisemakers. *Below,* a man sells white sand, which was used as absorbent material for animal waste as well as for gardening and for maintenance chores such as polishing metals. *Bottom,* a vendor of pickles and smoked eels.

"I do want to climb the tower," she said.

"You? What for? Did someone send you?" asked the old keeper.

"No. I want to see what I can see from the top."

"Be off with you," he told her, "and don't try your tricks on me again or it'll be the worse for you," and he began to shut the door. But Heidi caught hold of his coat.

"Let me go up just this once," she pleaded.

He looked down at her, and her eagerness softened him, so that he took her by the hand and said grumblingly, "Oh well, if it means so much to you, come along."

The boy made no move to go too, but sat down on the stone doorstep, waiting for her as she had asked him to. The door shut, and she and the old man climbed up

Here is the view that Heidi discovers from the top of the church. In the distance, to the right, is the cathedral tower. Most of the houses, with their small tiles and slate roofing, were destroyed during World War II and subsequently replaced by skyscrapers.

and up, the stairs getting narrower, the higher they went. At last they reached the top and the keeper held her up to an open window. "Now you have a good look round," he said. But still there was nothing to be seen but a sea of roofs, chimneys, and towers, and after a minute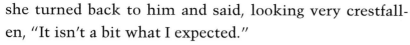

she turned back to him and said, looking very crestfallen, "It isn't a bit what I expected."

The typical cat is full of contradictions. It is very fond of fish but hates to get wet; it has a thick coat of fur but prefers to lie by the fireplace; and is an excellent climber but is sometimes unable to get down from a tree. Famous for its independence, the cat is a pet beloved by many.

"I thought as much! What does a little thing like you know about views! Come along now and don't ring any more tower bells."

He set her on the ground and she followed him down. When they came to the landing at the bottom of the narrowest flight of stairs she noticed a door on the left, which led to the keeper's room. There, in a corner beside it, a fat gray cat sat beside a big basket, and spat as Heidi approached, to warn her that this was the home of her family of kittens and that she would not allow anyone to meddle with them. Heidi stood and stared, for she had never seen such a huge cat before. There were such quantities of mice in the tower that it could catch half a dozen a day without any difficulty, and had grown sleek and fat on them.

"Come and look at the kittens," said the keeper. "The mother won't touch you if I'm with you." Heidi went up to the basket.

"Oh what darlings! Aren't they sweet?" she exclaimed with delight, as she watched seven or eight little kittens tumbling and scrambling over one another. "Would you like one?" asked the keeper, smiling at her pleasure.

"To keep for myself?" gasped Heidi, hardly able to believe her ears.

"Yes, of course. You can have more than one if you like, or indeed all of them if you've somewhere to keep them," said the old man, welcoming the opportunity of getting rid of them. Heidi was thrilled. There was plenty of room in the big house and she was sure Clara would love to have them.

"How can I carry them?" she asked, and stooped to pick one up, but the mother cat flew at her so fiercely that she drew back in alarm.

"I'll bring them to you, if you'll tell me where," said the old man as he stroked the cat soothingly. It had lived alone with him in the tower for many years and they were great friends.

"To Mr. Sesemann's house," Heidi told him, "where there's a gold dog's head with a ring in its mouth on the front door."

He recognized the house immediately from that description for he had lived in the one spot so long that he knew all the houses round about, and besides, Sebastian was a friend of his.

"I know the house," he said, "but for whom shall I ask? You don't belong to that family I'm sure."

"No, I don't, but I know Clara will be pleased to have the kittens."

The keeper was ready to go down the rest of the

way but Heidi couldn't tear herself away. "Can't I take just two kittens with me now," she begged, "one for me and one for Clara?"

"Wait a minute then," he said, and he picked up the mother cat and carried her into his room where he put her down in front of her food bowl. Then he shut the door and came back to the basket. "Now you can take them," he said.

Heidi's eyes were shining. She picked out a white kitten, and a tabby, and put one in each pocket. Then they went on down together and found the boy still sitting on the step, waiting for her.

"Now, which is the way back to Mr. Sesemann's house?" Heidi asked him as soon as the keeper had shut the big door behind her.

"Don't know."

Heidi described the house as well as she could, but the boy only shook his head.

"Well, opposite us, there's a gray house with a roof like this," she said, drawing gables in the air with one finger. He thought he recognized that, and ran off at once, with Heidi on his heels. Soon they reached the familiar door with the dog's head knocker. Heidi pulled the bell and almost at once Sebastian answered it. "Come in quickly," he cried as soon as he saw her, and he slammed the door without even noticing the boy, who was left outside feeling quite bewildered.

"Hurry, Miss," urged Sebastian. "They're already at table and Miss Rottenmeier looks fit to explode.

66 Then she saw a boy standing at a corner, with a hurdy-gurdy and a tortoise. 99

Whatever made you run away like that?"

She went into the dining room where there was an awful silence. Miss Rottenmeier did not look up as Sebastian pushed Heidi's chair up to the table, and even Clara did not speak. Then, looking very cross and speaking very severely, Miss Rottenmeier said:

"I will speak to you later, Adelheid. Now I will only say that it was extremely naughty of you to leave the house without asking permission or saying a word to anyone, and then to go roaming about until this late hour. I've never heard of such a thing."

"Meow," came the reply, which seemed to be Heidi's, and that was the last straw.

"How dare you mock me in such a fashion, and after such disgraceful behavior," said Miss Rottenmeier, her temper rising.

"I didn't," began Heidi, but got no further

66 Everything had quieted down and Clara had the kittens on her lap.99

before there was another "Meow, meow!" Sebastian almost threw what he was holding onto the table, and rushed from the room.

"That will do." Miss Rottenmeier tried to speak firmly, but she was almost choking with anger and could only whisper. "Leave the room."

Heidi got up, feeling quite frightened. She tried again to explain, but the kittens mewed again, "Meow, meow, meow."

"Heidi, why do you keep on mewing like that?" asked Clara. "Can't you see how angry you're making Miss Rottenmeier?"

"But it's not me, it's the *kittens*," Heidi managed to get out at last.

"What! Kittens! Here?" screamed Miss Rottenmeier. "Sebastian! Tinette! Come and look for the horrible creatures and get rid of them." And she rushed off into the study and bolted the door, for she disliked cats so much, she was actually terrified of them!

Sebastian was laughing so much, he had to wait outside the door to compose himself before he could come in. He had seen one of the kittens peeping out of Heidi's pocket as he was handing a plate, and knew there was bound to be trouble. When it started, he could not control his laughter and that was why he had rushed away. When he was in a fit state to come in again, everything had quietened down and Clara had the kittens on her lap. Heidi was kneeling beside her and they were both

A domestic scene from nineteenth-century Germany: the mistress of the house, wearing dark clothes, is seated at the head of the table. The girl at right—perhaps a daughter or niece—is wearing an ensemble inspired by the traditional peasant dress: a dirndl, an embroidered white shirt, and long braided hair. A maid looks on from a respectful distance. In back is one of the large stoves of white earthenware that for several centuries had been a favorite means of providing heat in the northern and eastern European countries. Inside it were long passageways of baked clay that retained the heat and allowed the stove to operate effectively on little fuel.

admiring the pretty little things.

"Sebastian, you must help us," said Clara. "Find a corner for the kittens where Miss Rottenmeier won't see them. She's scared of them and will certainly get rid of them if she finds them, but we want to have them to play with when we're alone. Where can we put them?"

"I'll see to that for you, Miss Clara," he said obligingly. "I'll make a cozy bed for them in a basket and put it where the old lady is not likely to look. You can rely on me." He went off to do as he had promised, chuckling to himself. He could foresee more excitements in the near future and always rather enjoyed watching Miss Rottenmeier in a rage. It was some time before that lady dared to open the study door. Then she called through a mere crack, "Are those dreadful creatures out of the way?"

"Yes, Ma'am," replied Sebastian, who was hanging about in the dining room, expecting that question. Then at once he snatched up the kittens and took them away.

The scolding which Miss Rottenmeier had intended to give Heidi had to be put off until next day, for she felt quite worn out with all she had been through of anxiety and annoyance, anger and fright. Consequently she withdrew very soon to her room, and Clara and Heidi went happily to bed, knowing that the kittens were safe.

8

STRANGE GOINGS-ON

" When quiet had been restored in the study, lessons were resumed.**"**

Next morning, just after Sebastian had opened the door to Mr. Usher and shown him into the study, the front door bell rang again, this time so loudly that Sebastian dashed downstairs thinking it must be Mr. Sesemann himself, come home unexpectedly. He flung open the door, and found there only a ragged boy with a hurdy-gurdy on his back.

"What's the meaning of this?" snapped Sebastian. "What do you want? I'll teach you to ring bells like that."

"I want to see Clara," said the boy.

"You dirty little brat, don't you even know enough to say 'Miss Clara'? And what can the likes of you want with her, anyway?"

"She owes me fourpence," was the reply.

"Rubbish! How do you even know that there is a Miss Clara in this house?"

"I showed her the way yesterday, for twopence, and then the way back for another twopence."

"You're telling lies," said Sebastian. "Miss Clara never goes out. She can't walk. Be off with you now, before I make you!"

The boy stood his ground, not in the least frightened by this threat. "I saw her in the street and I can tell you what she looks like," he said. "She's got short, curly black hair, black eyes, and she was wearing a brown dress and she doesn't talk like us."

"Oho," thought Sebastian with a grin. "The little miss again! What's she been up to this time? All right," he said aloud to the boy, "come with me," and he led the way to the study door. "Now wait here until I come back, then, when I let you in, you play a tune. Miss Clara will like that." He knocked and went in.

"There's a boy here who wants to speak to Miss Clara personally," he announced. Clara's eyes lit up at this highly unusual occurrence.

"Bring him in at once," she said. "He can come, can't he, Mr. Usher?"

The boy was in fact already in the

The hurdy-gurdy could be carried either on one's back or held in front over one's chest. Although it was first used exclusively by street musicians, it gradually came to be played in people's homes as well. Perhaps this couple is on their way to a musicale in a friend's drawing room.

room and began to turn the handle of his organ. Miss Rottenmeier had gone to the dining room to avoid having to listen to a child learning the alphabet. Suddenly she pricked up her ears. Was that noise coming from the street? It sounded nearer but—there could never be a hurdy-gurdy in the study! She ran to the door and there beheld the ragged street urchin calmly playing his organ. The tutor looked as though he wanted to say something, but couldn't make up his mind to, while Clara and Heidi were listening to the music with obvious pleasure.

Children of the middle class were often raised by a governess and educated by a tutor, and were liable to receive severe reprimands from these authority figures. Such a scenario was a favorite subject among illustrators of the time, as this rather satirical drawing shows.

"Stop, stop that at once!" cried Miss Rottenmeier, but it was difficult to make her voice heard above the noise. She darted toward the boy, and all but tripped over something on the floor. Looking down, she saw, to her horror, a queer dark object at her feet. It was the tortoise. She leaped in the air to avoid it—leaped, and she hadn't done that for years! Then she screamed at the top of her voice for Sebastian, and the boy stopped playing, for this time he heard her in spite of his music. Sebastian was standing just outside the door, doubled up with laughter. When at last he came in Miss Rottenmeier had collapsed on to a chair.

"Get rid of that boy and his animal at once," she ordered.

The little organ player snatched up his tortoise and

Sebastian led him away. On the landing, he put some coins into the boy's hand, saying, "Here's the money from Miss Clara, and a bit more for playing so nicely." Then he let him out at the front door.

When quiet had been restored in the study, lessons were resumed, but Miss Rottenmeier remained to prevent any more such unseemly happenings, and as she sat there, she made up her mind to find out what was at the bottom of it and to deal severely with whoever was responsible. Presently Sebastian came back to say that someone had just delivered a big basket which was to be given at once to Miss Clara.

"To me?" asked Clara in surprise, at once feeling most curious to know what it could contain. "Oh, bring it in at once." So Sebastian fetched in a closed basket, set it down before her, and went out again quickly.

"You had better finish your lessons before opening it," remarked Miss Rottenmeier firmly, though Clara looked longingly at it.

Then, in the middle of a declension, she broke off to ask Mr. Usher if she couldn't have just a peep inside.

"I could cite good reasons both for and against such a course of action," he began pompously. "In its favor is the fact that so long as your attention is entirely engaged . . ." He got no further. The lid of the basket was not properly fastened, and suddenly the room seemed to be swarming with kittens. They jumped out one after another and rushed madly about, some biting the tutor's trousers and jumping over his feet, others climbing up

66 Looking down, she saw, to her horror, a queer dark object at her feet. It was the tortoise. 99

114

Miss Rottenmeier's skirt. One scrambled onto Clara's chair, mewing and scratching as it came. The whole room was in an uproar, and Clara was delighted.

"Oh, aren't they pretty little things! Just look at them jumping about!" she exclaimed to Heidi, who was chasing after them from one end of the room to the other. Mr. Usher was standing by the table, trying vainly to shake the kittens off his legs. Miss Rottenmeier, disliking all cats as she did, only found her voice again after an interval, and then called loudly for Sebastian and Tinette. She was afraid that if she moved all the horrid little creatures would jump up at her. The servants

66 Suddenly the room seemed to be swarming with kittens.**99**

came quickly and Sebastian managed to catch the kittens and put them back into the basket. Then he carried them up to the attic where he had already made a bed for those Heidi had brought home the day before.

Once again Clara's lesson time had been far from boring. That evening, when Miss Rottenmeier had recovered a little from the morning's disturbance, she summoned Sebastian and Tinette to the study to question them about what had happened. Of course it came out that everything was the result of Heidi's escapade the day before. Miss Rottenmeier was so angry she could not at first find words to express herself. She sent the servants away and then turned to Heidi who was standing calmly beside Clara's chair, quite unable to understand what she had done wrong.

"Adelheid," said Miss Rottenmeier very sternly, "I can think of only one punishment for such a little savage as you. Perhaps a spell in the dark cellar among the bats and rats will tame you, and stop you having any more such ideas."

Heidi was very surprised at Miss Rottenmeier's idea of punishment. The only place she knew as a cellar was the little shed in which her grandfather kept their supplies of cheese and milk and where she had always been glad to go. And she had never seen any bats or rats.

Clara, however, protested loudly. "Oh, Miss Rottenmeier! Wait till Papa comes home! He'll be here quite soon, and I'll tell him everything and he'll decide what's to be done with Heidi."

> 66 Heidi was very surprised at Miss Rottenmeier's idea of punishment. The only place she knew as a cellar was the little shed in which her grandfather kept their supplies of cheese and milk and where she had always been glad to go. And she had never seen any bats or rats. 99

People kept cats not only because they enjoyed them as pets. Since refrigerators did not yet exist, mice and rats could boldly attack the foods stored in the larder; cats could perform a very useful household task.

Miss Rottenmeier could make no objection to this, and besides Clara must never be crossed.

"Very well, Clara," she said stiffly, "but I also shall speak to your father." With that she left the room.

The next few days passed uneventfully, but Miss Rottenmeier's nerves remained on edge. The sight of Heidi kept her reminded how she had been deceived over the child's age, and how she had so upset the household that it seemed as though things would never be the same again. Clara, on the other hand, was very cheerful and no longer found her lessons dull. Heidi always managed to provide some amusement. For one thing, she invariably got the letters of the alphabet so muddled up, it seemed as though she would never learn them, and when Mr. Usher tried to make things easier for her by comparing letters to familiar objects such as a horn or a beak, she thought of the goats at home, or the hawk on the mountain and that did not help her at all with her lesson.

In the evenings Heidi used to tell Clara about her life in the hut, but it made her feel so homesick that she often ended by exclaiming, "Oh I must go home again. I must go tomorrow." Clara tried to comfort her then by saying, "Stay at least until Papa arrives and then we'll see what will happen." Heidi seemed to cheer up at that, but secretly she was consoling herself with the thought that every day she stayed meant two more white rolls

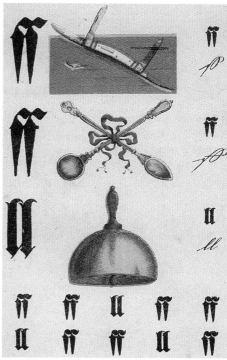

The illustration above helps to explain why Heidi had so much trouble learning to read. There is almost no difference among the letters *s*, *f*, and *l* in the Gothic script, in the words *Messer* (knife), *Löffel* (spoon), and *Schelle* (bell). "Making sticks," or learning to draw straight letters, was one of the first exercises that schoolchildren had to learn. It wasn't that easy, and writing neatly with a goose quill wasn't so simple either!

for Peter's Grannie. She had been putting them in her pocket at dinner and supper regularly since the day of her arrival and now had quite a pile hidden away. She wouldn't eat a single one herself, because she knew how much Grannie would enjoy them instead of her usual hard black bread.

> **"** So one afternoon she wrapped up the rolls and went downstairs. **"**

After dinner Heidi always sat alone in her room for a time. She had been made to realize that she could not simply run out-of-doors in Frankfurt as she had done at home, so she never tried again. Miss Rottenmeier had forbidden her to talk to Sebastian, and she would never have dreamed of starting a conversation with Tinette. Indeed she avoided her as much as possible for Tinette either spoke to her in the most disdainful way, or mimicked her, and Heidi knew quite well that she was being made fun of. So she had plenty of time every day to think how the snow would by now have melted on the mountain and of how beautiful it would be at home with the sun shining on the grass and the flowery slopes and over the valley below. She felt so homesick, she could hardly bear it. Then she remembered that her aunt had said she could go back if she wanted to. So one afternoon she wrapped up the rolls in her big red scarf, put on her old straw hat and went downstairs. But she had only got as far as the front door when she ran straight into Miss Rottenmeier returning from an outing. That forbidding person stared at Heidi in amazement and her sharp eyes came to rest on the red bundle.

"And what does this mean?" she demanded. "Why are you dressed up like that? Haven't I forbidden you to go running about the streets alone, or to go out without permission? Yet here I find you trying it again and looking like a beggar's child into the bargain."

"I wasn't going to run about," murmured Heidi, a little frightened. "I only want to go home to see Grandfather and Grannie."

"What's that? You want to go home?" Miss Rottenmeier threw up her hands in horror. "You'd simply run off like that? What would Mr. Sesemann say? I can only hope he'll never hear of it. What's wrong with this house, pray? Have you ever lived in such a fine place before, or had such a soft bed or such good food? Answer me that."

"No," said Heidi.

"You have everything you can want here. You're an ungrateful little girl who doesn't know when she's well off."

This was too much for Heidi and she burst out, "I want to go home because while I'm here Snowflake will be crying, and Grannie will be missing me too. And here

This well-brought-up little girl feels sorry for having hurt her doll. Dolls were thought of as educational toys: they helped a young girl become familiarized with the role of wife and mother—a role it was assumed she would someday fulfill. According to a child's mood, the doll was either lavished with attention or made to suffer, as though it had feelings.

119

I can't see the sun saying good night to the mountains. And if the hawk came flying over Frankfurt he'd croak louder than ever because there are such a lot of people here being horrid and cross, instead of climbing high up where everything's so much nicer."

"Merciful heavens! The child's out of her mind!" exclaimed Miss Rottenmeier and ran swiftly upstairs, bumping violently into Sebastian who was going down. "Bring that wretched child up here at once," she ordered.

"Very good," said Sebastian.

Heidi hadn't moved. She was trembling all over and her eyes were blazing. "Well, what have you done this time?" asked Sebastian cheerfully. Still she didn't stir, so he patted her shoulder and added sympathetically, "Come now, don't take it so much to heart. Keep smiling, that's the best thing to do. She bumped into me so hard just now she nearly knocked my head off. But don't you worry. Come along. We've got to right-about-turn and upstairs again. She said so." Heidi went slowly with him, looking so very dejected that Sebastian felt really sorry for her.

"Cheer up," he said, "don't be downhearted. I've never seen you cry yet and I know you're a sensible little girl. Later on, when Miss Rottenmeier's out of the way, we'll go and look at the kittens, shall we? They're having a fine time up in the attic and it's fun to

This illustration, which is from a children's fashion magazine of the end of the nineteenth century, shows us just how sophisticated were the clothes of rich children at the time. Like their mothers, little girls wore hats and carried umbrellas; underneath their low-waisted dresses were petticoats. The second figure from the left, a boy, wears a sailor suit, which was practically the "uniform" of all little boys at the time. William II (the German emperor and King of Prussia from 1888 to 1918) is thought to have started the fashion when he was a child by wearing the sailor suit given to him by his grandmother, Queen Victoria of England. Jumping rope was a favorite game, as was rolling a hoop.

watch them playing together."

Heidi gave a subdued little nod and went to her room, leaving him looking after her with real kindliness.

At supper Miss Rottenmeier hardly spoke, but every now and then she glanced sharply at Heidi as though expecting her to do something unheard of at any moment. But the little girl sat as quiet as a mouse, eating and drinking nothing, though she managed to put her roll in her pocket as usual.

Next morning, when Mr. Usher arrived, Miss Rottenmeier beckoned him mysteriously into the dining room and told him she feared the change of air and the new way of life, with all its unusual experiences, had affected Heidi's mind. She told him how the child had tried to run away and repeated the extraordinary things she had said. Mr. Usher tried to calm her.

"I assure you," he said, "that although in some ways Adelheid is rather peculiar, in others she seems quite normal and it should be possible, with careful treatment, to steady her quite satisfactorily in the end. I am really more worried by the fact that she seems to find such difficulty in learning the alphabet. So far we have made no progress at all."

Miss Rottenmeier felt somehow satisfied by that and let him go to his pupils. Later in the day she remem-

These are examples of the clothes worn by children in the late 1800s. Beginning at the upper left: a "day shirt," a dress, a tunic for a little boy, underpants for a girl, a cape and a matching bonnet. The quantity of embroidery, all of it done by hand, is remarkable in today's world of mass production. Boys wore a tunic like the one shown here until they were old enough to go to the "gymnasium" or secondary school.

bered the strange garments Heidi had put on to go home in, and decided she ought to give her some of Clara's outgrown clothes before Mr. Sesemann came home. She spoke to Clara about it and she agreed at once that Heidi could have several of her dresses, hats, and other garments. So Miss Rottenmeier went off to Heidi's room to look at her clothes and decide what was worth keeping and what should be thrown away. In a few minutes she returned, looking more put out than ever.

"Adelheid" she cried, "what do I find in your wardrobe? Can I believe my eyes? Just think of it, Clara, at the bottom of the cupboard—a cupboard meant for clothes, Adelheid—I found a great pile of stale dry rolls. Fancy hoarding food away like that!" Then she raised her voice and called Tinette. "Go to Miss Adelheid's room," she told her, "and get rid of the rolls in the cupboard, and throw the old straw hat that's on the table into the dustbin!"

"Oh, no," Heidi wailed, starting up, "I must keep my hat, and the rolls are for Grannie." She tried to run after Tinette but Miss Rottenmeier caught hold of her.

"You'll stay here. That rubbish is going to be thrown away," she said firmly.

Heidi threw herself down beside Clara's chair and began to cry bitterly. "Now

From his dress and demeanor, it is clear that this servant is being portrayed as not far below his employer in status. At once a butler, confidant, and chief steward, this is the stereotypical servant who frequently has an important role in novels and plays. He knows he is his master's equal in intelligence and ability, even if his fortune and position are less exalted.

Grannie won't get any nice white bread," she sobbed. "The rolls were all for her and now they're going to be thrown away." She wept as if her heart would break, and Miss Rottenmeier hurried out of the room. Clara was very upset by all the commotion.

"Heidi, don't cry so," she begged. "Listen to me. If you'll only stop, I promise to get you just as many rolls as you had saved, or even more, to take to Grannie when you go home. And they'll be soft, fresh ones. Those you'd saved must have got quite hard already. Come on, Heidi, please don't cry any more."

It was a long time before Heidi could stop, but she understood what Clara was promising and was comforted at last, though she still wanted to be assured that Clara meant it.

Judging by his harried aspect and the livery, or uniform, he wears, this servant has apparently been relegated to performing the lesser duties, such serving meals. His master is sure to be displeased by the careless way he is carrying the bottle.

"Will you really give me as many rolls as I had saved?" she asked in a still tearful voice.

"Of course I will. Now do cheer up."

Heidi came to supper that night with red eyes, and when she saw the roll beside her plate, a lump came in her throat. But she managed not to cry for she knew that would not do at table. Sebastian kept making strange signs whenever he came near her, pointing first to his head, then to hers, nodding and winking as he did so, as though to convey to her something very secret, and when she went to bed she found her battered old straw hat under the quilt. She caught it up and squashed it a little more in her pleasure at seeing it again. Then she wrapped it up in a big old handkerchief and hid it right at the back of the wardrobe.

That was what Sebastian had been trying to tell her at supper. He had heard what Tinette had been told to do, and had heard Heidi's despairing cry. So he had gone after the girl and waited till she came out of Heidi's room carrying the hoard of rolls, with the hat perched on top of them. He had snatched away the hat, saying, "I'll get rid of this," and so had been able to save it.

66 When she went to bed she found her battered old straw hat under the quilt.**99**

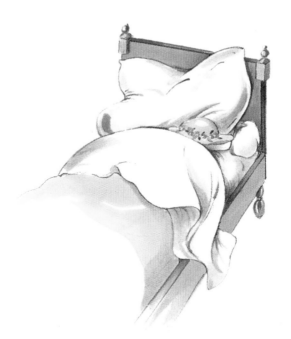

9

A BAD REPORT TO MR. SESEMANN

❝ 'Have you brought me nice cold water, my dear?' 'Straight from the fountain'**❞**

There was a great bustle in the big house and much running up and down stairs a few days later, for the master had returned from his travels, and Sebastian and Tinette had one load of luggage after another to carry up from the carriage, for Mr. Sesemann always brought a lot of presents and other nice things home with him.

The first thing he did was to go and find his daughter, and there was Heidi with her, for it was the late afternoon, when they were always together. Father and

Here, some leather goods from the nineteenth century. At top is a satchel, in the center is a canteen. The third item is a leather kit containing toilet items such as nail-care implements and bottles for lotions. It is likely that when Mr. Sesemann traveled he took with him a toilet kit like this. It was an expensive purchase at the time and would only have been affordable to the wealthy.

daughter were very fond of one another and they greeted each other very warmly. Then he put out a hand to Heidi, who had moved quietly away into a corner, and said kindly:

"So this is our little Swiss girl. Come and shake hands. That's right. And tell me, are you and Clara good friends? I hope you don't squabble, so that you have to kiss and make it up and then start the whole performance again."

"No, Clara is always good to me," said Heidi.

"And Heidi never quarrels with me," added Clara.

"I'm glad to hear that," said her father. "And now, my dear, you must forgive me if I leave you. I haven't had anything to eat all day. But I'll come back later on and you shall see all that I've brought for you."

He went along to the dining room, where Miss Rottenmeier was making sure that everything was in order. There he sat down and she took a seat opposite him, with a face like a thundercloud.

"What's the matter?" he asked. "Why this gloomy expression to welcome me home, when Clara seems in such good spirits?"

"Mr. Sesemann," she began pompously, "we have all been dreadfully deceived, Clara not least of us."

"Indeed?" he returned calmly, sipping his wine.

"You remember we agreed that Clara should have a young companion to live with her? Knowing how careful you are that she should only have about her well behaved, nicely brought up people, I thought a young Swiss girl from the mountains would be suitable. I've often read of these girls, who float through the world like a breath of pure Alpine air; almost, as it were, without touching the ground."

"I think even Swiss children must put their feet on the ground if they want to get anywhere," remarked Mr. Sesemann drily, "otherwise they'd have been given wings."

"Oh, that's not what I meant," she cried. "You know a real child of nature, hardly touched by this world at all."

"I don't quite see what use that would be to Clara," observed Clara's father.

"I'm serious, Mr. Sesemann. I have been disgracefully imposed upon!"

"What's disgraceful about it? I see nothing in the child herself to be so upset about."

"You should see the sort of people and animals she has been bringing into the house. Mr. Usher will bear me out about that. And that's not all."

"I don't understand you," he said. But now Miss Rottenmeier saw that she had his attention.

"I don't wonder. Her conduct in general has been almost past belief. I can only think she's not quite right in the head."

Mr. Sesemann had not taken her earlier complaints seriously, but this was another matter and, if true, Clara might come to some

At left is a wallet, most likely made of snakeskin. *Below*, a page from a travel catalog, whose items include "dust-hiding" clothes. Horse-drawn carriages and steam-powered trains would often leave travelers at the end of the day coated in dust or grimy from the soot of the coal furnace. The ladies' outfit consisted of a bustled dress, with the inner whalebone framework that gave women the distinctive figure that was highly prized during its day. Indispensable items for the men included a small case for guidebooks (such as the famous Baedecker) and another for cigars.

harm. He looked at the woman as though wondering whether she herself was quite right in the head, and at that moment the door opened and Mr. Usher was announced.

"Just the man we want," declared Mr. Sesemann. "Come and sit down, and have a cup of coffee. You'll be able to clear things up for me, I'm sure. Tell me plainly what you think of my daughter's little companion. What's all this about her bringing animals into the house? Do you think she's at all odd?"

The tutor began to explain in his roundabout fashion that he had only come to say how glad he was that Mr. Sesemann had returned safely, but the compliments were waved aside. Mr. Sesemann wanted a quick answer to his questions. But still Mr. Usher began his explanations, as though he was something which had been wound up and had to go on till the works ran down.

"If I am to express an opinion about the young person," he said, "I should like first of all to emphasize that, though she may be backward in some respects as a result of a rather neglected—or perhaps I should say late—education, and because of her prolonged sojourn in the mountains, which of course could be beneficial in itself, if not of too long duration . . ."

"My dear Mr. Usher," interrupted Mr. Sesemann, "don't bother about such details. Just tell me whether you have been alarmed by her bringing animals into the house and what you think of her in general as a companion for my daughter."

"I should not like to say anything against the child," Mr. Usher replied

The tortoise is a reptile that, although incapable of rapid movement, has survived since prehistoric times thanks to its extraordinary toughness and long life span. The shell designed to protect it, however, almost caused its extinction, as tortoiseshell became a valuable ornamental material—for such items as hair clips, eyeglass frames, and hand mirrors—and remained in great demand until the advent of the first plastics in the early 1900s.

carefully, "for if, on the one hand, her conduct is somewhat unconventional as a result of her primitive way of life before she came to Frankfurt, this change is for her, I make bold to say, undoubtedly important and . . ."

Mr. Sesemann got up. "Excuse me, Mr. Usher, don't let me disturb you, but I must just get back to my daughter." He hurried out and did not return, but went to the study and sat down beside Clara. Heidi stood up when he entered the room and as he wanted her out of the way for a few minutes, he said:

It is not unusual for a cat to give birth to seven or eight kittens in a single litter. This puts the cats' owner in the difficult position of having to decide what to do with them.

"My dear, will you go and fetch me—now whatever was it I wanted?—oh yes, a glass of water."

"Fresh water?"

"Yes, fresh cold water." Heidi vanished.

He pulled his chair closer to his daughter and stroked her hand. "Now Clara dear, I want you to tell me about these animals your little playmate has been bringing into the house, and why does Miss Rottenmeier think she is not quite right in the head?"

Clara told him just what had happened, about the tortoise and the kittens, the rolls and everything. When she had finished, her father laughed heartily.

"Well well, then you don't want me to send her home, Clara? You're not tired of her?"

"Oh no, Papa," she cried. "Since Heidi's been here, delightful things have happened nearly every day. It's much more amusing, and she tells me all

129

sorts of interesting things."

"That's all right then. And here comes your little friend. Have you brought me nice cold water, my dear?"

"Straight from the fountain," said Heidi, handing it to him.

"But you didn't go to the fountain all by yourself?" said Clara.

"Yes I did. And I had to go a long way, because there were so many people round the first two fountains that I had to go on to the next street and fetch it from there. And I met a gentleman with white hair and he sent his kind regards to Mr. Sesemann."

"Well, you've had quite a journey," said Mr. Sesemann with a smile. "I wonder who the gentleman was."

A major thoroughfare during the reign of the Williams: the emperors Wilhelm I (who ruled from 1871–88) and his son Wilhelm II (who ruled from 1888–1918). In fact, this is the Kaiserstrasse, which means "imperial street." When the Prussians won the war against the French in 1870, they demanded payments in gold—payments that financed an era of great public projects. Following the lead of the great administrator Baron Haussmann in Paris, wide avenues were cut through German cities and lined with magnificent houses; horse-drawn carriages could pass several abreast, and an army march by on parade. The new streets were also better lit, had monumental fountains and statues, and boasted the first of the new department stores. The trolley cars indicate that this photograph was taken after Heidi's time.

"He stopped by the fountain and said, 'As you've got a glass, please give me a drink. Who are you fetching the water for?' And I said, 'For Mr. Sesemann.' Then he laughed and said he hoped you would enjoy it."

"Describe him to us," said Mr. Sesemann.

"He had a nice smile, and wore a thick gold chain with a gold thing hanging on it which had a red stone in the middle. And he had a stick with a horse's head handle."

"The doctor," cried Clara and her father with one voice, and he smiled at the thought of what his old friend would have to say about this unusual search for water to quench his thirst.

That evening, he told Miss Rottenmeier, as they were discussing household matters, that Heidi was to stay. "The child seems perfectly normal and Clara loves having her here," he explained. "You mustn't regard her funny little ways as faults, and I want you, please, to make sure that she's always kindly treated. If you find her too much to manage on your own—well, you'll have some help soon for my mother will be coming for her usual long visit and she can manage anyone, as you know."

"Yes indeed, Mr. Sesemann," replied Miss Rottenmeier, rather crestfallen, for she did not particularly relish this news.

Mr. Sesemann was only at home a fortnight, then had to go to Paris on business. Clara was very disappointed that he could not stay longer, and to cheer her up he told her about her grandmother's promised visit, and almost as soon as he had left, a letter came to say that old Mrs. Sesemann was on her way, and would arrive on the following day. She asked for the carriage to be sent to fetch her from the station.

Clara was delighted, and talked so much about Grandmamma that Heidi began to speak of her as Grandmamma too. Miss Rottenmeier frowned when she heard her, but the little girl was so used to seeing disapproval on that face that she did not pay much attention to it. But as she was going to bed that night, Miss Rottenmeier called her and told her she was never to address Mrs. Sesemann as "Grandmamma." "You must call her 'Gracious Madam.' Do you understand?" Heidi was puzzled, but encountered such a forbidding look in the lady's eye that she did not like to ask her why.

Here, some fashionable men from the late nineteenth century. Many of the popular styles were heavily influenced by the fashions in England, as can be seen from the checked trousers, and were quite formal and uncomfortable by today's standards. This was true at any rate for the privileged classes, who signaled in this way that they did not have to do physical labor. For example, the shirts have high, starched collars that inhibit free movement of the neck and head. A suit, such as worn by the gentleman in the middle, along with a top hat, were the only respectable clothes for a man to go out in, right up until 1914: as one etiquette book put it, "A man who steps out of his home must never part with his hat, neither when visiting, nor at a dinner in town, nor at the ball." A cane was an equally essential accessory. Yet under the influence of the English sporting spirit, a certain degree of comfort began to be tolerated, particularly for traveling, hunting, or going to the country. One might wear a soft hat and a large caped coat, called a macfarlane, such as Sherlock Holmes wore.

66 The carriage came rolling up to the front door.99

10

GRANDMAMMA'S VISIT

Next day everyone was very busy preparing for the expected guest. It was easy to see that she was an important person in that household and was accustomed to being treated as such. Tinette put on a nice new cap in her honor. Sebastian collected all the footstools he could find and put them in convenient places so that she would find one ready wherever she sat down. Miss Rottenmeier fussed about the place, inspecting everything, as though determined to show her authority and that she did not mean to be deprived of any of it by the new arrival.

As the carriage came rolling up to the front door,

Sebastian and Tinette ran downstairs. Miss Rottenmeier followed in a more dignified fashion to receive the guest. Heidi had been told to stay in her room until she was sent for, so that Clara and her grandmother could have a little while alone. So Heidi sat there, quietly saying over to herself the words with which she had been told to address the old lady. They sounded so strange to her that she rearranged them, thinking Miss Rottenmeier must surely have made a mistake, and that "Madam" must come first. Before long Tinette stuck her head round the door, and said sharply, "You're to go to the study."

Heidi did as she was told, and as she came into the room, Mrs. Sesemann said in a friendly voice, "Come over here, my dear, and let me have a good look at you."

Heidi went to her and said clearly and carefully, "Good evening, Madam Gracious."

"What was that?" laughed the old lady. "Is that how you address people up in the mountains?"

"No, no one's called that at home," said Heidi gravely.

"Nor here either. In the nursery I'm always just 'Grandmamma' and that's what you shall call me too. You'll remember that all right, won't you?"

"Yes, I've used that name."

"Good," said Grandmamma, with an understanding nod, patting her cheek. Then she looked closely at her and nodded again, liking what she saw, for the child's eyes were grave and steady as they looked back, and Heidi saw such a kind expression on the old lady's face that she loved her at once. Indeed everything about Grandmamma was delightful to Heidi. She had pretty white hair and wore a dainty lace cap, with two broad ribbons which fluttered behind, as though there was always a gentle breeze blowing round her. Heidi thought that specially attractive.

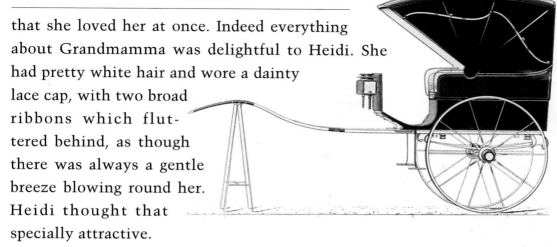

"And what's your name?" Grandmamma asked.

"My real name's Heidi, but now it's supposed to be Adelheid, so I answer if I'm called that." At that moment Miss Rottenmeier came into the room and Heidi stopped in confusion, remembering that she was still so unaccustomed to her full name that she frequently did not answer when that lady called her by it.

"I'm sure you'll agree, Mrs. Sesemann," said the disagreeable woman, "that it is better to call her by a name that can be used without embarrassment, especially to the servants."

"My good Rottenmeier," replied Mrs. Sesemann, "if she's always been called Heidi and is used to that name, I shall certainly call her that."

Miss Rottenmeier

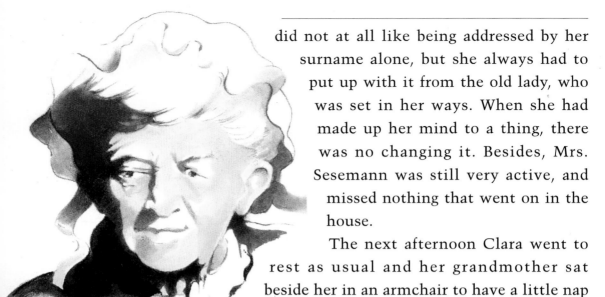

did not at all like being addressed by her surname alone, but she always had to put up with it from the old lady, who was set in her ways. When she had made up her mind to a thing, there was no changing it. Besides, Mrs. Sesemann was still very active, and missed nothing that went on in the house.

The next afternoon Clara went to rest as usual and her grandmother sat beside her in an armchair to have a little nap too. After it, she felt quite refreshed, and went along to the dining room to find the housekeeper, but the room was empty.

"Perhaps she's having a little sleep too," she thought, and went on to Miss Rottenmeier's bedroom and knocked sharply on the door. It was opened after a moment by that lady, who looked rather taken aback at sight of her visitor.

"I just want to know where Heidi is, and what she does with herself in the afternoons," said Mrs. Sesemann.

"She sits in her room," Miss Rottenmeier replied. "She might be doing something useful if she had the least inclination that way, but instead she makes the most ridiculous plans and even tries to carry them out—things I could really hardly mention in polite society."

"Depend upon it I should do exactly the same, if I were left alone like that. And probably you wouldn't care to mention my ideas in polite society either. Go and bring her to my room. I want to give her some books I've brought with me."

"Books!" exclaimed Miss Rottenmeier, clasping her hands together. "Books are no use to her! In all the time she has been here, she hasn't even learned her alphabet. It seems quite impossible to teach her, as Mr. Usher will tell you. If he hadn't the patience of a saint, he would have given her up long ago."

"That's strange. The child doesn't look stupid. Go and fetch her anyway. She can at least look at the pictures." Miss Rottenmeier wanted to say something more, but Mrs. Sesemann turned and quickly left her room. She was very surprised to hear that Heidi was so slow to learn and made up her mind to find out why. She had no intention of asking Mr. Usher, however. She knew he was quite a good man, and she always made a point of greeting him very politely when they happened to meet, but she took good care not to land herself in conversation with him as she found his pompous way of expressing himself quite unbearable.

Heidi soon came to her, and was delighted to have the beautiful big picture books to look at. Then, all of a sudden, she gave a little cry and burst into tears. Mrs. Sesemann glanced at the picture which had upset her, and saw that it was of a green meadow where many

This colored lithograph, or "chromo," shows an idyllic mountain scene. On the left is a chamois hunter dressed in the nineteenth-century Alpine style, with his Tyrolean hat, short hunting jacket, leather shorts with wide, embroidered suspenders, and an alpenstock, or alpinist's walking stick. On the right, two children watch their goats, as Heidi and Peter do; and in the back is a chalet.

Mountaineers in Switzerland, Bavaria, and Austria continue wearing traditional clothing to this day. Key components of the outfit are the richly embroidered leather shorts called lederhosen, a walking stick, and sturdy shoes. Over the calf, a sort of stocking with no foot is worn. Alpinists returning from the mountains used to feel honorbound to bring back edelweiss, the white, furry flowers pictured in the foreground. Nowadays they are so rare that it is absolutely forbidden to pick them, under penalty of a stiff fine.

animals grazed, watched over by a shepherd leaning on a long staff. The sun was setting and the meadow was bathed in golden light. She patted Heidi's hand and said in a very kind voice:

"Come child, don't cry. I suppose it reminded you of something. But there's a nice story to it, which I'll tell you this evening, and there are lots of other stories in the book to read. Now dry your eyes for I want to talk to you. Sit here where I can see you properly."

It was some time before Heidi could stop crying, and Mrs. Sesemann let her alone while she composed herself. As she grew calmer, the old lady said, "That's right. Now we can have a nice little talk. First tell me, child, how you are getting on with your lessons. What have you learned?"

"Nothing," said Heidi, with a sigh, "but I knew I should not be able to."

"What do you mean by that? What is it you don't think you can learn?"

"To read. It's too difficult."

"What makes you think that?"

"Peter said so, and he ought to know because he's tried and tried but he just can't learn."

"He must be a very odd boy then. But you mustn't simply take his word for it. You must try hard yourself. I don't think you can have paid proper attention to Mr. Usher's lessons."

"It's no use," said Heidi in a hopeless tone.

"Now listen to me, Heidi, you've never learned to

read because you believed what Peter told you. Now you must believe what I say, that in a little while you will be able to read quite well, as most children do, being on the whole like you and not like Peter. And as soon as you can read, you shall have the book with the picture of the shepherd in the meadow for your very own, and then you'll be able to read the story for yourself and find out what happens to him and his animals. You'd like that, wouldn't you?"

Heidi had been listening eagerly, with shining eyes. Then she sighed and exclaimed, "I wish I could read now!"

"It won't take you long, I'm sure," Grandmamma told her. "Now we must go and see Clara. Let us take the books with us." And hand in hand they went to the study.

A change had come over Heidi since the day she had tried to go home and Miss Rottenmeier had given her such a scolding. She now understood that, in spite of what Detie had told her, she could not go away when she wanted to, and that she would have to stay in Frankfurt for a long time, perhaps forever. She believed that Mr. Sesemann would think her very ungrateful if she said she wanted to go away, and probably Grandmamma and Clara would think the

Snakes and ladders was one of the favorite family games of the period. This one portrays the triumphs and disasters of an expedition into the mountains. At the time of *Heidi*, the mountains, previously considered inhospitable obstacles to man's progress, were suddenly "discovered" as a place of profound natural beauty and adventure. It became fashionable to roam through the Alps, and to take cures there for one's health. The Swiss writer and illustrator Rodolphe Toepffler (1799–1846) became famous for the notebooks he kept of his travels in the Alps.

same, if they knew. So she dared not tell anyone how she felt, but went about mournfully, with a heavy heart. She had begun to lose her appetite and grew quite pale. When she was alone in her quiet room at night, she often lay awake for hours, thinking of home and the mountains, and when she fell asleep at last, it was to dream of them so vividly that she woke in the morning expecting to run joyfully down the ladder from the loft—and found herself, after all, still in the big bed in Frankfurt, so far away. The disappointment of that awakening often made her cry miserably, burying her face in her pillow so that no one should hear.

Grandmamma saw her unhappiness but said nothing for a few days, waiting to see if it would pass. When there was no improvement, and she had noticed traces of tears on the little face on several mornings, she took Heidi into her room and asked very kindly what the matter was and why she was so sad.

Heidi was afraid of vexing her if she told her the truth, and answered, "I can't tell you."

"Can't? Could you tell Clara then?"

"Oh no, I can't tell anyone," said Heidi so sadly that the old lady's heart ached for her.

"Listen to me," she said, "if we're in trouble and can't tell any ordinary person, why, there is always God whom we can tell, and if we ask Him to help us, He always will. Do you understand? You do pray to God every night, don't you, to thank Him for all the good things and to ask Him to protect you from harm?"

"No, I don't," was the reply, "never."

"Haven't you been taught to pray, Heidi? Don't you know how?"

"I used to pray with my own grandmother, but that's a long, long time ago. I've almost forgotten about it."

"Ah—and when you are sad, and have no one to turn to for help, can't you see what a comfort it is to tell God all about it, knowing that He will help? Believe me, He always finds some way of making us happy again."

Heidi's eyes brightened. "May I tell Him everything, really everything?" she asked.

"Yes, everything."

Heidi slipped her hand out of the old lady's.

"May I go now?" she asked.

"Of course, child."

She ran to her own room, sat down on her stool, and folded her hands. Then she poured out all her troubles to God and begged Him to help her to get home to her grandfather.

One morning, about a week later, Mr. Usher asked if he might speak to Mrs. Sesemann on an important matter. He was invited to her room, where she received him in her usual friendly way.

"Come in and sit down, Mr. Usher," she said. "I'm

For many, religion played a very important part in a child's upbringing. Saying grace at meals and a bedtime prayer at night were daily activities in most families. For some children, religion answered their need for wonder, and allowed them to confide, make wishes, and dream.

Below is a scene from a middle-class household in the early 1800s. Families tended to be larger than they are today, and a typical household often included unmarried aunts or cousins and grandparents.

An afternoon of studying at home. Until this century, books were extremely expensive, and so owning them was a sign of considerable affluence.

pleased to see you. What is it you want to speak to me about? No complaints, I hope?"

"On the contrary, Madam," he replied. "Something has come to pass which I had long given up hoping for. Indeed I think no one who knew the facts would have expected it. Yet, there it is—the impossible has happened."

"Are you going to tell me that little Heidi has learned to read at last?" asked Mrs. Sesemann. The young man opened his eyes very wide.

"Why, that you should suggest such a possibility, Madam, is almost as surprising as the fact itself. Up till now, in spite of all my efforts, she seemed quite unable to learn even the letters, and I had reluctantly come to the conclusion that she would have to be left to try to learn them in her own way, without any further help from me. Now she has mastered them almost overnight, as it were, and *can read*—and more correctly than most beginners. It's really remarkable."

"There are many strange things in this life," agreed Mrs. Sesemann, well pleased. "Perhaps this time there was a new desire to learn. In any case, let us be thankful the child has got thus far, and let us hope she will continue to make progress."

She then went with the tutor to the door and, as he went downstairs, hurried to the study to find out for herself about this good news. She found Heidi reading aloud to Clara, and quite excited at the new world which had been opened to her, as the black letters on the page came alive and turned into stories about all kinds of people and things.

This soberly dressed woman—most likely a governess—dictates while her charge writes. Competence in spelling and handwriting was considered the sign of a good education.

That evening, at supper, Heidi found the big picture book beside her place. She looked brightly at Grandmamma, who nodded and said, "Yes, it's yours now."

"For ever and ever? Even when I go home?" asked Heidi, flushing with pleasure.

"Yes, of course, and tomorrow we'll start to read it."

"But you won't be going home, Heidi, not for ages," put in Clara. "Grandmamma will be leaving soon and then I shall need you more than ever."

Before going to sleep that night, Heidi had a good look at her lovely book, and thereafter, reading was her greatest delight. Sometimes in the evening Grandmamma would say, "Now Heidi shall read to us," and that made her very proud. She seemed to understand the stories better when she read them aloud, and Grandmamma was always ready with any explanation that was necessary. Her favorite story, which she constantly re-read, was about the shepherd whose picture had brought the tears to her eyes when she first saw it. Now she knew it showed him happily

A little girl reads to her grandmother while the older woman sips at her cherries in brandy. They are both huddled together under the light of a kerosene lamp. Before incandescent lamps were invented by Thomas Edison in 1879, houses were not very well lit at night. Wax candles were used until the middle of the last century, when they were replaced by kerosene lanterns. These constantly needed to be refilled. To save on fuel, the only lamp lit was often the one in the living room, and everyone would draw close to catch its meager rays. Reading in those circumstances had a certain charm: one sat in a pool of yellow with darkness all around.

tending his father's sheep and goats in sunny meadows, like those on the mountain. In the next picture he had left his good home and was minding a stranger's pigs in a foreign land. Here the sun was not shining and the countryside was gray and misty. The young man looked pale and thin in that picture, for he had nothing but scraps to eat. The last one showed his old father running with outstretched arms to greet him as he returned home sorrowful, and in rags.

With so many nice stories to read and pictures to look at, the days of Grandmamma's visit passed happily, but all too quickly.

11

HOMESICKNESS

Every afternoon during Mrs. Sesemann's visit, while
Clara was resting and Miss Rottenmeier had taken herself off mysteriously, presumably to rest also, the old
lady sat with her granddaughter for a few minutes, and
then called Heidi to her room, where she talked to her
and amused her in a variety of ways. She had some pretty little dolls with her and showed Heidi how to make
clothes for them, and in this pleasant fashion the child
learned to sew, almost without realizing it. Mrs.
Sesemann had a wonderful piece bag, with materials of

all kinds and colors in it, and from these Heidi made dresses, coats, and aprons for the dolls. Sometimes Mrs. Sesemann let her read aloud from her book, which of course pleased her very much, and the more often she read the stories the more she liked them. She lived with the characters and got to know them all so well, she was always glad to meet them again. But in spite of these pleasant distractions, she did not look really happy, and her eyes had quite lost their sparkle.

One afternoon during the last week of Grand-mamma's stay, Heidi came to her room as usual, with the big book, and the old lady drew her to her side, laid the book down, and said:

"My dear, tell me why you're not happy. Is it still the same trouble?"

Heidi nodded.

"Did you tell God about it?"

"Yes."

These children have dropped their costly toys and dolls to play horsey on their brother's back. The games that children invent themselves are often the ones they like most. King Henry IV of France (1553–1610) is said to have played horsey with his children while the ambassadors of Spain waited at his door.

"And do you pray to Him every day to make you happy again?"

"No, not any more."

"I'm sorry to hear that. Why have you stopped?"

"It's no use," Heidi told her. "God didn't hear me and I daresay that if all the people in Frankfurt pray for things at the same time, He can't notice everybody and I'm sure He didn't hear me."

146

"Why are you so sure?"

"I prayed the same prayer every day for a long time and nothing happened."

"It isn't quite like that, Heidi. God is a loving Father to us all and knows what is good for us. If we ask for something it isn't right for us to have, He won't give it to us, but in His own good time, if we go on praying and trust in Him, He'll find us something better. You can be sure it's not that He didn't hear your prayer, for He can listen to everybody at once. That's part of the wonder of it. You must have asked for something He thought you ought not to have at present and probably said to himself, 'Heidi's prayer shall be answered but only at the right moment so that she will really be happy. If I answer it now perhaps later on she'll wish she hadn't asked for it, because things may not turn out as she expects.' He has been watching over you all this time—never doubt that—but you have stopped praying, and that showed you did not really believe in Him. If you go on like that, God will let you go your own way. Then if things go wrong and you complain that there's no one to help you, you will really have only yourself to blame, because you will have turned your back on the one Person who could really help you. Do you want that to happen, Heidi, or will you go now at once and ask God to forgive you and help you to find more faith, to help you to go on praying every day, and to trust Him to make things come right for you in the end?"

Just as they sometimes do now, dolls in the nineteenth century often had luxurious wardrobes. It was not unusual for little girls to learn to sew by making costumes for their dolls. These came in a wide variety, from homemade rag dolls to dolls made of wax, leather, and porcelain, with real eyelashes and real hair applied one strand at a time—true works of art for the children of the rich. Toys intended for boys had a definite military orientation: they included soldiers made of lead or papier-mâché, and toy swords, guns, and drums. Toy horses and carriages were also supposed to prepare the little man for his future responsibilities.

A woman and her daughter at the window, watching the goings-on in the street below. In those days—before the advent of radio, television, and the automobile—many people spent a great deal of time at the window or in the street, exchanging news and gossip.

Heidi had listened very carefully to all this. She had great confidence in Grandmamma and wanted to remember everything she said, and at the end she cried, penitently:

"I will go at once and ask God to forgive me and I'll never forget Him again."

"That's a good girl."

Heidi went to her own room then, much encouraged, and begged God not to forget her but to give her His blessing.

The day of Grandmamma's departure was a sad one for Clara and Heidi, but she managed to keep them happy right up to the moment when she drove off in the carriage. It was only when the sounds of the wheels died away, and the house was so quiet and empty, that the children felt quite forlorn and did not know what to do with themselves.

Next evening Heidi came into the study carrying her book and said to Clara, "I'll read to you a lot now, if you'd like me to." Clara thanked her, and Heidi began the little task she had taken on herself with enthusiasm. But all did not go smoothly, for the story she had chosen proved to be about a dying grandmother. It was too much for Heidi who burst into tears and sobbed, "Grannie is dead." Everything she read was so real to her that she was firmly convinced that it was Peter's Grannie in the story.

"Now I shall never see her again," she wept, "and she never had one of the nice white rolls."

Clara had great difficulty in persuading her that the story was about quite another grandmother, and even when she began to understand that, she was not comforted for it had made her realize that Peter's Grannie might really die, and her grandfather too, while she was so far away, and that if she did not go home for a long time, she might arrive to find everything changed and her loved ones gone forever.

Miss Rottenmeier came into the room during this scene, and as Heidi went on crying, she looked at her very impatiently and said, "Adelheid, stop howling like that and listen to me. If I ever hear you making such a to-do again while you're reading to Clara, I'll take the book away from you and you shan't have it again."

This threat had an immediate effect, for the book was Heidi's greatest treasure. She turned quite pale, quickly dried her eyes, and stifled her sobs. She never wept again after that, no matter what she read, but the effort it cost her sometimes produced such queer grimaces that Clara was quite astonished. "I've never seen anything like the faces you're making," she used to say. But at least Miss Rottenmeier did not notice anything, and once Heidi had got over one of her spells of sadness, everything would go smoothly for a time.

This child daydreams while doing his homework. Slates were often used for writing, since they provided a surface that could be used over and over again. Paper was very expensive.

Her appetite did not improve, however, and she looked very thin and peaky. It quite upset Sebastian at mealtimes to see her refuse even the most delicious things. As he handed them to her, he would sometimes whisper, "Just try some of this, Miss, it's so good. That's not enough. Here, take another spoonful." But all in vain. She ate hardly anything. And when she was in bed and all the well-loved scenes of home came before her eyes, she cried and cried, until her pillows were quite wet.

Time went by, but in the town Heidi scarcely knew whether it was winter or summer. The walls and houses, which were all she could see from the windows, always looked the same, and now she only went out-of-doors when Clara was feeling well enough for a drive. Even then they saw nothing but bricks and mortar, for Clara could not stand a long excursion and they only drove round the neighboring streets, where they saw plenty of people and beautiful houses, but not a blade of grass or a flower or a tree, and no mountains. Heidi's homesickness grew on her from day to day, till just reading the name of some well-loved object was enough to bring tears to her eyes, though she would not let them fall.

Autumn and winter passed and the bright sunlight shining again on the white walls of the house opposite set Heidi guessing that soon Peter would be taking the goats up to pasture again, and that all the flowers would be in bloom and the mountains ablaze with light each evening. When she was in her own room, she used to sit with her hands over her eyes to shut out the town sunshine, and would stay like that, forcing back her overwhelming homesickness until Clara wanted her again.

This maid is going to sit by the bed of a sick person. In one hand she carries a metal shovel for picking up hot coals, and in the other hand a little brazier to put them in. The invalid can then warm his or her feet on the brazier.

12

THE HOUSE IS HAUNTED!

66 John and Sebastian settled down and immediately opened the wine which soon made them talkative. Then they grew sleepy and lolled back in their armchairs and fell into a doze. 99

Strange things began to happen in that house in Frankfurt. Miss Rottenmeier had taken to wandering silently about it, deep in thought; and if she had to go from one room to another or along the passages after dark, she often looked over her shoulder or peered into corners, as if afraid that someone might creep out of the shadow, and pluck at her skirt. If she had to go upstairs to the richly furnished guest rooms or down to the great drawing room, in which footsteps echoed at the best of times and where old councillors in stiff white collars

The stoves used in those days were of cast iron, and were sometimes enameled like the one shown here. They were very bulky by modern standards, but these big stoves were the kitchen's centerpiece, the place where fragrant soups simmered, potatoes fried, and bacon sizzled, filling the room with mouthwatering aromas. One filled a stove with wood or coal by lifting off the rings on the stovetop, and it served as both a cooking range and a water heater. The most advanced models also had a hot-water reservoir and a plate warmer.

stared out from the portraits on the walls, she always made Tinette go with her—in case there should be anything to carry up or down. Strange to say, Tinette behaved in much the same way. If she had to go to those rooms, she got Sebastian to go with her, on the same pretext of helping to carry something. And Sebastian seemed also to feel the same way. If he was sent into any of the unused rooms, he called John the coachman and asked him to go too—in case he could not manage the job alone. And everyone did as they were asked and went along too, without any fuss, though their help was never really needed. It looked as if they all thought that they might want assistance themselves some time. Down in the kitchen things were no better. The old cook, who had been there a long time, stood by her saucepans, shaking her head and muttering, "That I should live to see such goings on."

The reason for all this uneasiness was that for some time past the servants had been finding the front door wide open every morning when they came down, but there was never anything to show who had opened it. For the first day or two the house had been thoroughly searched to see whether anything had been stolen, for it was thought a burglar might have hidden himself during the day and made off with his booty during the night. However, nothing was missing. Then they double-locked the front door and bolted it every night, but still they found it wide open in the morning, no matter how early the servants came down.

At last, Miss Rottenmeier persuaded John and Sebastian to spend a night downstairs in the room next to the drawing room, to see if they could discover the cause of the mystery. They were provided with weapons belonging to Mr. Sesemann, and a bottle of wine to fortify them for whatever might happen.

When evening came they settled down and immediately opened the wine which soon made them talkative. Then they grew sleepy and lolled back in their armchairs and fell into a doze. The clock striking twelve brought Sebastian to his senses and he said something to John but John was fast asleep and only settled himself more comfortably into his chair at each effort to rouse him. Sebastian, however, was wide awake now, and listening for unusual sounds. But none came, either from the house or from the street. In fact, the silence was so deep that he grew uneasy. He saw it was no use trying to wake John by calling to him so he shook him, but another hour passed before John was really awake and remembered what he was there for. He got to his feet then, with a fine show of courage, and said:

Many contemporary houses are designed with an open, airy kitchen easily accessible and in sight of the dining room. In Heidi's time, since kitchens were places for servants, they were hidden; often they were located at the rear of the house, reachable by a service staircase that led on to the servants' quarters above.

"We'd better go and see what's going on. Don't be afraid. Just follow me."

He pushed open the

door, which had been left ajar, and went out into the passage. Almost at once the candle in his hand was blown out by a gust of wind from the front door which was standing wide open. He rushed back into the room at that, almost knocking Sebastian over, and slammed the door and locked it. Then he struck a match and lit the candle again. Sebastian did not know what had happened. John was portly enough to block his view completely and he had seen nothing. He had not even felt the draft. But John was white as a sheet and trembling like an aspen leaf.

❝ Miss Rottenmeier sat down and wrote very emphatically to Mr. Sesemann, telling him to come home at once.❞

"What's the matter? What was outside?" Sebastian asked anxiously.

"The front door was wide open," John told him, "and there was a white figure on the stairs which suddenly vanished."

A cold shiver ran down Sebastian's spine. They sat down close together and did not stir thereafter until it was broad daylight and they could hear people going by in the street. Then they went and shut the front door and then reported to Miss Rottenmeier. They found her already up and dressed, for she had been awake most of the night wondering what they would discover. As soon as she had heard their story, she sat down and wrote very emphatically to Mr. Sesemann, telling him she was so paralyzed with fright she could hardly hold a pen, and must beg him to come home at once as no one in the house could sleep easily in their beds for fear of what might happen next.

The answer, by return of post, said that it was not possible for Mr. Sesemann to leave his business and return home so precipitately. He was surprised to hear of a "ghost" about the house, and hoped it was only some temporary disturbance. However, if the trouble continued, he suggested that Miss Rottenmeier should write and ask his mother to return to Frankfurt. She would certainly know how to deal with any "ghosts" effectively, so that they did not show themselves again. Miss Rottenmeier was annoyed that he did not take the matter more seriously. She wrote immediately to Mrs. Sesemann, but got no satisfaction from this quarter either. The old lady replied somewhat tartly that she had no intention of traveling all the way to Frankfurt again because Rottenmeier imagined she had seen a ghost. There had never been a "ghost" in the house, and in the old lady's opinion, the present one would prove to be very much alive. If Rottenmeier could not deal with the matter herself, the letter went on, she should send for the police.

Miss Rottenmeier was not inclined to endure much more, and she had a shrewd idea how to make the

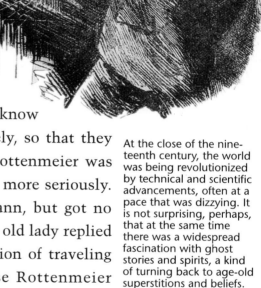

At the close of the nineteenth century, the world was being revolutionized by technical and scientific advancements, often at a pace that was dizzying. It is not surprising, perhaps, that at the same time there was a widespread fascination with ghost stories and spirits, a kind of turning back to age-old superstitions and beliefs.

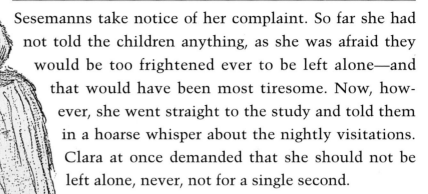

A ghost, as drawn by the person it appeared to. Though this ghost drags no rusty chains, it does wear a cape that looks like the shroud—a white sheet—that was traditionally thought to be worn by phantoms.

Sesemanns take notice of her complaint. So far she had not told the children anything, as she was afraid they would be too frightened ever to be left alone—and that would have been most tiresome. Now, however, she went straight to the study and told them in a hoarse whisper about the nightly visitations. Clara at once demanded that she should not be left alone, never, not for a single second.

"Papa must come home. You must sleep in my room," she cried. "Heidi mustn't be left alone either, in case the ghost does anything to her. We'd better all stay together in one room and keep the light on all night, and Tinette will have to sleep in the next room and John and Sebastian had better be out in the corridor so that they can frighten the ghost away if it comes upstairs." Clara was thoroughly worked up by that time, and Miss Rottenmeier had great difficulty in calming her.

"I'll write at once to your papa," she promised, "and put my bed in your room so that you're never alone. But we can't all sleep in one room. If Adelheid is frightened Tinette shall put up a bed in her room." But Heidi was much more afraid of Tinette than of ghosts, of which indeed she had never heard, so she said she was not frightened and would sleep alone in her own room. Miss Rottenmeier then went to her desk and wrote dutifully to Mr. Sesemann to let him know that the mysterious happenings in the house still continued, and were threatening to have a very bad effect on Clara in her delicate state of health. "Fright might even send her into fits," she wrote, "or bring on an attack of St. Vitus' dance."

Her plot was successful. Two days later Mr. Sesemann stood at his front door, ringing the bell so vigorously that everyone jumped, thinking the ghost had started playing tricks by daylight. Sebastian peeped through one of the upstairs windows to see what was happening, and at that moment the bell rang again so loudly that there could be no real doubt that a human hand had pulled it. He realized that it was his master and rushed downstairs, almost falling head over heels in his haste. Mr. Sesemann hardly noticed him, but went at once to Clara's room. She welcomed him joyfully and he was greatly relieved to find her so cheerful and, to all appearances, much as usual. Clara assured him she was really no worse, and was so pleased to see him that she felt quite grateful to the ghost for bringing him home.

"And how has the 'ghost' been behaving, Miss Rottenmeier?" he asked that lady with a smile.

"Oh, it's a serious matter," she replied stiffly. "I don't think even you will be laughing about it tomorrow. It seems to me that something terrible must have happened here some time in the past, though it has not come out until now."

"I must ask you not to cast reflections on my entirely respect-

The famous French doctor Claude Bernard (1813–1878) claimed he had never encountered a patient's soul under his surgical knife. The question of whether the spirit survives after death, in part a religious question, is still asked nonetheless; mediums and psychics try to hold conversations with the dead. The picture below illustrates their theory that the soul survives death: we see the white shape of a soul rising from a body.

This large, finely worked candlestick serves both to light a table and to decorate it festively.

This gold object is a bottle holder, of the kind found on richly laid tables. It is used to serve wine.

able forebears!" said Mr. Sesemann. "Now please send Sebastian to me in the dining room. I want to talk to him alone." He had noticed that Sebastian and Miss Rottenmeier were not exactly on the best of terms and that gave him an idea.

"Come here," he said, as Sebastian entered, "and tell me the truth. Did you play the ghost to frighten Miss Rottenmeier?"

"Oh, sir, please don't think that. I'm just as frightened as she is," replied Sebastian, and it was plain that he was speaking the truth.

"Well, if that's the case, I shall have to show you and the worthy John what ghosts look like by daylight. A great strong chap like you ought to be ashamed of running away from such a thing. Now I want you to take a message to Dr. Classen. Give him my regards and ask him to come and see me without fail at nine o'clock tonight. Say I've come back from Paris on purpose to consult him, and that the matter is so serious that he'd better come prepared to spend the night. Is that clear?"

"Yes, sir. I'll see to it at once."

Mr. Sesemann then went back to tell his daughter that he hoped to lay the ghost by the next day.

Punctually at nine o'clock, when both children were in bed and Miss Rottenmeier had retired for the night, the doctor arrived. Although his hair was gray, he had a fresh complexion and his eyes were bright and kind. He looked rather worried when he came in, but as soon as he saw his friend, he burst out laughing.

"I must say you look pretty well for a man wanting someone to sit up all night with you!" he said, patting him on the shoulder.

"Not so fast, my friend," replied Mr. Sesemann. "Your attention is likely to be needed all right, and by someone who won't look as well as I do when we've caught him."

"So there really is a patient in the house," returned the doctor, "and one who has to be caught, eh?"

"Much worse than that! We've a ghost! The house is haunted."

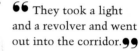
66 They took a light and a revolver and went out into the corridor. 99

The doctor laughed out-right.

"You're not very sympathetic," objected Mr. Sesemann. "It's a good thing Miss Rottenmeier can't hear you at the moment. She's firmly convinced one of my ancestors is prowling around, doing penance for his sins."

"How did she come to meet him?" asked the doctor, still chuckling.

Mr. Sesemann told him all he knew, and added, "To be on the safe side I've put two loaded pistols

159

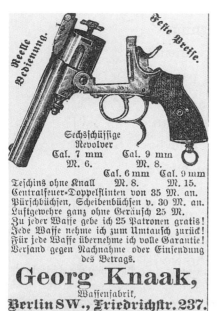

This is an advertisement for a revolver, which is simply a pistol with a revolving cylinder.

Wine making has ancient roots in Germany. Mostly white wine is produced, which sometimes is fermented like champagne to make a sparkling wine.

in the room, where you and I are going to keep watch. I've a feeling it may be a very stupid practical joke which some friend of the servants is playing in order to alarm the household during my absence. In that case a shot fired into the air to frighten him will do no harm. If, on the other hand, burglars are preparing the ground for themselves by making everyone so afraid of the 'ghost' that they won't dare to leave their rooms, it may equally be advisable to have a good weapon handy."

While he was talking, Mr. Sesemann led the way to the same room where John and Sebastian had spent the night. On the table were the two guns and a bottle of wine, for if they had to sit up all night, a little refreshment would certainly be welcome. The room was lit by two candelabra, each holding three candles. Mr. Sesemann had no intention of waiting for a ghost in the dark, but the door was shut so that no light should penetrate into the corridor to give warning to the ghost. The men settled themselves comfortably in their armchairs, for a good chat and a drink. Time passed quickly and they were quite surprised when the clock struck midnight.

"The ghost's got wind of us and isn't coming," said the doctor.

"We must wait a while yet," replied Mr. Sesemann. "It isn't supposed to appear till about one o'clock."

So they chatted on, for another hour. In the street outside everything was quiet, when suddenly the doctor raised a warning finger. "Did you hear anything, Sesemann?" he asked.

They listened and heard distinctly the sound of a bolt being pushed back, and a key turned, then the door opened. Mr. Sesemann reached for his revolver.

"You're not afraid, are you?" asked the doctor quietly.

"It's better to be careful," the other whispered back.

They each took a light in one hand and a revolver in the other and went out into the corridor. There they saw a pale streak of moonlight coming through the open door, and shining on a white figure which stood motionless on the threshold.

"Who's there?" shouted the doctor so loudly that his voice echoed down the corridor. They both moved toward the front door. The figure turned and gave a little cry. It was Heidi who stood there, barefooted, in her white nightgown, staring in bewilderment at the weapons and the lights. She began to tremble and her lips quivered. The men looked at each other in astonishment.

"Why I believe it's your little water-carrier!" said the doctor.

"What are you doing here, child?" asked Mr. Sesemann. "Why have you come downstairs?"

Heidi stood before him, white as her nightgown, and answered faintly, "I don't know."

"I think this is a case for me," said the doctor. "Let me take the child back to her room, while you go and sit down again." He put his revolver on the ground, took Heidi gently by the hand, and led her

Until the nineteenth century, a clock was a sign of affluence. Like this one, they were often encased in a sumptuous cabinet. Thanks to a simplified mechanism and wide-scale production, they became less expensive, and spread to a wider portion of the population—even the countryfolk.

upstairs. She was still shivering and he tried to soothe her by speaking in his friendly way to her. "Don't be afraid. Nothing terrible is going to happen. You're all right."

When they reached her room, he set the light down on the table and lifted Heidi back into bed. He covered her up carefully, then sat down in a chair beside her and waited until she was more herself. Then he took her hand and said gently, "That's better. Now tell me where you were going."

"Nowhere," whispered Heidi. "I didn't know I'd gone downstairs. I just was there."

Her small hand was cold in the doctor's warm one.

"I see," he said. "Can you remember whether you'd had a dream? One perhaps that seemed very real?"

"Oh yes." Heidi's eyes met his. "I dream every night that I'm back with Grandfather and can hear the wind whistling through the fir trees. I know in my dream the stars must be shining brightly outside, and I get up quickly and open the door of the hut—and it's so beautiful. But when I wake up I'm always still here in Frankfurt." A lump came in her throat and she tried to swallow it.

"Have you a pain anywhere?" asked the doctor. "In your head or your back?"

"No, but I feel as though there's a great stone in my throat."

"As though you'd taken a large bite of something and can't swallow it?"

Heidi shook her head. "No, as if I wanted to cry."

"And do you sometimes have a good cry?"

Her lips quivered again. "No. I'm not allowed to. Miss Rottenmeier has forbidden it."

"So you swallow it down, I suppose. You like being in Frankfurt, don't you?"

"Yes," she said, but it sounded much more as though she meant to say No.

"Where did you live with your grandfather?"

"On the mountain."

"That wasn't much fun, was it? Didn't you find it rather dull there?"

"Oh no, it's wonderful." Heidi got no further. The memory of home, added to the shock of all she had been through, overcame the ban which had checked her tears, and they suddenly rained down her cheeks and she sobbed bitterly.

This advertisement from the end of the nineteenth century is for a new gadget to trim lamp wicks. The wick hung down into a reservoir filled with kerosene. One raised it by turning a small wheel. After a time, the wick got charred, which made the lamp smoke and turned the lamp glass and the ceiling black with soot. As a result, the wick needed to be trimmed often. Today, of course, we simply flick a switch to get light!

The doctor got up and laid her head gently on the pillow. "Have a good cry, it won't do you any harm," he said. "Then go to sleep, and in the morning everything will be all right." He left the room and went to find Mr. Sesemann, who was anxiously awaiting him.

"Well, in the first place your little foster child is a sleepwalker," he began. "Without knowing anything about it, she has been opening the front door every night and frightening the servants out of their wits. In the second place she's terribly homesick, and appears to have

Unlike Heidi, who walks in her sleep, this child seems to be sleeping in perfect peace. It was approximately in Heidi's time that an Austrian doctor, Sigmund Freud (1856–1939), began to be interested in unconscious activities such as dreaming and sleepwalking. His first subjects were often children, as he found a child's unconscious mind generally easier to access than that of an adult.

lost a great deal of weight, for she's really not much more than skin and bone. Something must be done at once. She's very upset and her nerves are in a bad state. There's only one cure for that sort of trouble—to send her back to her native mountains, and immediately. She should leave for home tomorrow—that's my prescription."

Mr. Sesemann got to his feet and paced up and down the room, much disturbed. "Sleepwalking, homesick, and losing weight—fancy her suffering all this in my house without anyone noticing! She was so rosy and strong when she arrived. Do you think I'm going to send her back to her grandfather looking thin and ill? No, you really mustn't ask me to do that. Cure her first. Order whatever you like to make her well, then I'll send her home, if she wants to go."

"You don't know what you're talking about," protested the doctor. "This is not an illness that can be cured with pills and powders. The child's not robust, but if you send her back to the mountains at once she'll soon be herself again. If not . . . you might find you have to send her back ill, incurable, or even not at all."

Mr. Sesemann was greatly upset. "If that's how things are, doctor, of course I'll do as you say," he promised.

When at last the doctor took his leave, it was the light of dawn which flooded through the front door.

13

HOME AGAIN

66 She was lifted into the carriage, the basket and a bag of provisions were handed up, then Sebastian got in. 99

Mr. Sesemann went upstairs feeling both anxious and annoyed, and he knocked loudly on Miss Rotten-meier's door. She awoke with a start to hear him say, "Please get up quickly and come to the dining room. We have to make preparations for a journey." She looked at her clock: its hands pointed to only half past four. She had never got up so early in her life. What could have happened? She was in such a state of curiosity and excitement that she hardly knew what she was doing, and kept looking for garments which she had already put on.

Mr. Sesemann then went along the passage and pulled vigorously at the bells which communicated with the rooms where the servants slept. Sebastian, John, and Tinette all leaped out of bed and threw on their clothes just any how, thinking the ghost must have attacked their master and that he was calling for help. They sped to the dining room one after the other, all rather dishevelled, and were taken aback to find Mr. Sesemann looking as brisk and cheerful as usual, and not at all as though he had seen a ghost. John was dispatched to fetch the carriage and horses at once, Tinette to waken Heidi and get her ready for a journey. Sebastian was sent to fetch Detie from the house where she worked.

Meanwhile Miss Rottenmeier completed her toilet, though she had put on her cap the wrong way round, so that from a distance it looked as though she were walking backward, but Mr. Sesemann rightly attributed this to her having been disturbed so early. He wasted no time on explanations, but told her to find a trunk immediately, and pack all Heidi's belongings in it. "Put some of Clara's things in as well," he added. "The child must be well provided for. Hurry, now, there's no time to lose."

Miss Rottenmeier was so astonished that she just stood and stared at him. She had been expecting him to tell her some terrible story about the ghost (which she would not have minded hearing by daylight).

Instead she was met with these extremely business-like (if rather inconvenient) orders. She could not understand it, and simply waited blankly for some sort of explanation. But Mr. Sesemann left her, without saying anything further, and went to Clara's bed-

Basel is one of the largest cities in the German-speaking part of Switzerland. Through its center flows the Rhine, which is still close to its source at that point. Basel's cathedral is famous, as is its very ancient university. The city's residents enjoy maintaining Basel's special traditions—their annual carnival, for instance, is celebrated in a solemn, dignified way, unlike most carnivals which are lively, sometimes riotous events.

room. As he expected, she had been awakened by all the commotion and was most anxious to know what had happened, so he sat down at her bedside and told her the whole story, ending up, "Dr. Classen is afraid Heidi's health has suffered, and says she might even go up on the roof in her sleep. You can understand how dangerous that would be. So I've made up my mind that she must go home at once. We can't risk anything happening to her, can we?"

Clara was very distressed at this news and tried hard to make her father change his mind, but he stood firm, only promising that if she was sensible and did not make a fuss, he would take her to Switzerland the following year. Then, seeing there were no two ways about it, she gave in, but she begged that, as a small consolation, Heidi's trunk should be brought to her room to be packed, so that she could put in some nice things which Heidi would like. To this her father willingly agreed.

By this time Detie had arrived and was wondering uneasily why she had been sent for at such an unearthly hour. Mr. Sesemann repeated to her what he had learned about Heidi's condition. "I want you to take her home at once, this very day," he said. Detie was very upset, remembering how Uncle Alp had told her never to show her face again upon the mountain. To have to take Heidi back to him like this, after the way she had carried her off, was asking too much of her.

"Please do excuse me," she said glibly, "but it is not possible for me to go today, nor yet tomorrow. We're very busy, and I really couldn't even ask for the day off just now. Indeed, I don't quite know when I could manage it."

Mr. Sesemann saw through her excuses, and sent her away without another word. He told Sebastian instead to prepare himself at once for a journey.

"You'll take the child as far as Basle today," he said, "and go on with her to her home tomorrow. I'll give you a letter for her grandfather so there will be no need for you to explain anything and you can come straight back here. When you get to Basle, go to the hotel whose name I've written on this visiting card. I'm well known there, and when you show it you'll be given a good room for the child, and they'll find a room for you too. And now listen to me," he went on, "this is very important. You must make sure all the windows in her room are shut

Many buildings during Heidi's time were heated very little or not at all, and anyone who sat still needed to be warmly clothed. This explains the wool cap and dressing gown that were worn in offices, a custom that today would seem very strange. The quill pen was held between the teeth or in the inkwell to avoid making blots. Special powders were used to dry the ink (these were later replaced by blotting paper), and mail was sealed with melted sealing wax, which was heated over a candle flame and stamped with a seal.

securely so that she can't open them. Then, once she's in bed, you are to lock her bedroom door on the outside for she walks in her sleep, and in a strange house it might be very dangerous if she wandered downstairs and tried to open the front door. Do you understand?"

"So that's what it was," exclaimed Sebastian, as the truth suddenly dawned upon him.

"Yes, that was it. You're a great coward and you can tell John he's another. You made fine fools of yourselves, all of you!" And with that Mr. Sesemann went to his study to write to Uncle Alp. Somewhat shamefaced, Sebastian muttered to himself, "I wish I hadn't let that idiot of a John push me back into the room, when he saw the figure in white! If only I'd gone after it. I certainly would if I saw it now." But of course by that time the sun was lighting up every corner of the room.

Meanwhile Heidi was waiting in her bedroom, dressed in her Sunday frock and wondering what was going to happen. Tinette considered her so far beneath her notice that she never threw her two words where one would do, and she had simply wakened her, told her to dress, and had taken her clothes out of the wardrobe.

When Mr. Sesemann came back to the dining room with his letter, breakfast was on the table. "Where's the child?" he asked, and Heidi was at once fetched, and came in, giving him her usual "Good morning."

"Well, child, is that all you have to say?" he inquired.

She looked at him questioningly.

"I do believe nobody's told you," he said with a smile. "You're going home today."

"Home," she gasped, so overwhelmed that for the moment she could hardly breathe.

"Well? Aren't you pleased?"

"Oh yes, I am," she said fervently, and the color came into her cheeks.

"That's right. Now you must eat a good breakfast," and he took his place at the table and signed to her to join him. She tried hard but couldn't swallow even a morsel of bread. She was not sure whether she was awake or still dreaming, and might not find herself presently standing at the front door again in her nightgown.

"Tell Sebastian to take plenty of food with him," Mr. Sesemann said to Miss Rottenmeier, as that lady came into the room. "The child is not eating anything at all—and that is not to be wondered at." He turned to Heidi. "Now go to Clara, my child, and stay with her until the carriage arrives." That was just what Heidi wanted to do, and she found Clara with a big trunk open beside her.

"Come and look at the things I've had put in for you," Clara cried. "I hope you'll like them. Look, these frocks and aprons and hankies and some sewing things. Oh, and this!" Clara held up a basket. Heidi peeped and jumped for joy, for inside were twelve beautiful rolls

Europe was revolutionized by the railroad in the nineteenth century. Distances that before had seemed vast were now easily traveled. Goods and people could be swiftly transported from one place to another, and the pace of communication was greatly speeded up. It was truly the advent of the modern age. Here, the magnificent train station in Frankfurt.

for Grannie. In their delight the children quite forgot that they were so soon to part, and when they heard someone call, "The carriage is here," there was no time to be sad. Heidi ran to the room which had been hers, to fetch the book which Grandmamma had given her. She always kept it under her pillow, for she could never bear to be parted from it, so she felt sure no one would have packed it. She put it in the basket. Then she looked in the cupboard and fetched out her precious old hat. Her red scarf was there too, for Miss Rottenmeier had not thought it worth putting in the trunk. Heidi wrapped it round her other treasure and put it on top of the basket where it was very conspicuous. Then she put on a pretty little hat which she had been given, and left the room.

66 Heidi was sitting in the train, with the basket on her lap. **99**

She and Clara had to say good-bye quickly, for Mr. Sesemann was waiting to put Heidi in the carriage, and Miss Rottenmeier was standing at the top of the stairs to say good-bye too. She saw the funny-looking red bundle at once, and snatched it out of the basket and threw it on the floor. "Really, Adelheid," she scolded, "you can't leave this house carrying a thing like that, and you won't need it anymore. Good-bye." After that Heidi did not dare to pick it up again, but she gave Mr. Sesemann an imploring look.

"Let the child take what she likes with her," he

said sharply. "If she wanted kittens and tortoises too, there would be no reason to get so excited, Miss Rottenmeier."

Heidi took up her precious bundle, her eyes shining with gratitude and happiness. "Good-bye," said Mr. Sesemann, shaking hands before she got into the carriage. "Clara and I will often think of you. I hope you'll have a good journey."

"Thank you for everything," said Heidi, "and please thank the doctor too, and give him my love." She remembered that the doctor had said that everything would be all right the next day, so she was sure he must have helped to make this come true. She was lifted into the carriage, the basket and a bag of provisions were handed up, then Sebastian got in.

"Good-bye and a pleasant journey," Mr. Sesemann called after them, as the carriage drove off.

Soon Heidi was sitting in the train, with the basket on her lap. She would not let go of it for an instant, because of the precious rolls inside. Every now and then she peeped at them and sighed with satisfaction. For a long time she spoke never a word, for she was only beginning to realize that she was really on her way home to Grandfather, and would see the mountains and Peter and Grannie. As she thought about them all, she suddenly grew anxious, and asked, "Sebastian, Peter's Grannie won't be dead, will she?"

Ringed with towering glaciers, the Austrian village of Grindenwald soon became a popular railroad stop in the summer. People liked to go mountain climbing and to ride the extraordinary funicular—a cable railway—up the sides of the Wetterhorn mountain. It was built in 1908.

"Let's hope not," he replied. "She'll be alive all right, I expect."

Heidi fell silent again, looking forward to the moment when she would actually give the rolls to her kind old friend. Presently she said again, "I wish I knew for certain that Grannie's still alive."

"Oh, she'll be alive all right. Why shouldn't she be?" said Sebastian, who was nearly asleep. Soon Heidi's eyes closed too. She was so tired after her disturbed night and early rising that she dozed off, and slept soundly till Sebastian shook her by the arm, crying, "Wake up. We have to get out here. We're at Basle."

For several hours more next day they continued their journey by train, and Heidi still sat with the basket on her lap. She would not let Sebastian take it, even for a moment. She was very silent, but inside she grew more and more excited. Then, just when she was least expecting it, she heard a voice calling, "Mayenfeld, Mayenfeld." She and Sebastian jumped up in surprise, and scrambled out on the platform with the trunk. Then the train went puffing on down the valley and Sebastian looked after it with regret. He preferred traveling comfortably and without effort, and did not look forward to climbing a mountain. He felt sure it would be very dangerous, and the country seemed to him only half-civilized. He looked about for someone to tell them the safest way to Dörfli, and near the station entrance he noticed a small cart to which a skinny pony was harnessed. A big man was carrying out to it some heavy sacks which had come

This village lies at 6,500 feet (2,000 meters) in the Simplon Pass, which crosses over the Alps between Switzerland and Italy. In 1906, the Simplon Tunnel was opened and the small Swiss town of Brigue was linked by twelve miles (twenty kilometers) of road to the town of Iselle in Italy. This was the first direct road between northwest Europe and Italy.

Mountain chalets were built of wooden boards and roofed with split shingles, giving many of them an irregular though picturesque appearance. The various parts of these structures—the rafters, beams, joists, and lintels—were worked with hand tools, giving a distinctively rough, simple look to the high mountain villages.

off the train, and to him Sebastian put his question.

"All the paths here are safe," was the answer. That did not satisfy Sebastian, who went on to ask how they could best avoid falling down precipices, and how to get a trunk up to Dörfli. The man glanced at it, then said, "If it's not too heavy, I'll take it on my cart. I'm going to Dörfli myself."

After that it was a short step to persuade him to take Heidi, as well as her trunk, with him and to send her on the last part of the journey up the mountain with someone from the village.

"I can go alone. I know the way all right from there," Heidi put in, after listening attentively to the conversation. Sebastian was delighted at having got out of the climb. He took Heidi to one side and gave her a fat packet and a letter for her grandfather. "The packet's for you, a present from Mr. Sesemann," he said. "Put it at the bottom of the basket and see you don't lose it. He'd be very angry if you did."

"I won't lose it," said Heidi, tucking both letter and packet away. She and her basket were then lifted on to the driver's seat, while the trunk was placed in the back of the cart. Sebastian felt rather guilty, as he knew he was meant to take her all the way home. He shook hands with her and reminded her with warning signs to remember what he had just given her. He was careful not to mention it out loud in the hearing of the driver. Then the man swung himself up beside Heidi, and the cart rolled off toward the mountain, while Sebastian returned to the little station to wait for a train to take him home.

The man on the cart was the baker from Dörfli, who had been to collect some flour. He had never seen Heidi, but like everyone in the village he had heard of her. He had known her parents and realized at once who she was. He was surprised to see her back again and was naturally curious to find out what had happened, so he began to talk to her.

"You must be the little girl who used to live with Uncle Alp, your grandfather, aren't you?" he inquired.

"Yes," said Heidi.

"Did they treat you badly down there, that you're coming so soon?"

"Oh no," Heidi cried. "Everyone was very kind to me in Frankfurt."

"Then why are you coming back?"

"Mr. Sesemann said I could come."

"I'd have thought you would rather have stayed if you were so well off there."

"I'd a million times rather be with Grandfather on the mountain than anywhere else in the world," she told him.

"Perhaps you'll change your mind when you get there," muttered the baker, thinking to himself, "It's a rum business, but she must know what it's like."

He began to whistle then, and said no more. Heidi

When winter ends and the snows have melted, it is time to do some maintenance on the houses. The floors and roof have to be strengthened or repaired, and the parts that have carried the heavy weight of the snow—the beams, ridge pole, and rafters—need to be tested for strength. Over the years, the wood turns dark, with hints of brown and gray, and hardens from being repeatedly wet.

looked around with growing delight at the mountain peaks she knew so well and which seemed to greet her like old friends. She wanted to jump down from the cart and run the rest of the way, but she managed to sit still, though she was shivering with excitement. They reached Dörfli just as the clock struck five, and there was soon a little crowd of villagers round the cart, curious to find out about the child and the trunk which had come in on it.

Because wood is a natural material that has varied characteristics and colors, it can be used for many kinds of projects. It can be seasoned and strengthened by dipping it in chemical solutions or allowing it to air-dry over a long period. White woods, such as willow, beech, and birch, were traditionally favored by the cooper in making casks and barrels, while the softness, strength, and flexibility of resinous woods such as the pine, fir, and larch recommended them to those who made sculpted ornaments.

The baker lifted Heidi down. "Thank you," she said hastily. "Grandfather will come and fetch the trunk," and she turned to run off home at once, but the villagers crowded round her, with a string of questions. She struggled through them, looking so pale and anxious that they murmured among themselves, as they let her go, "You can see how frightened she looks, and no wonder," and they added, "If the poor child had anywhere else in the world to go, she'd never come running back to that old dragon." The baker, aware that he was the only person who knew anything on that subject, now spoke up. "A gentleman brought her to Mayenfeld and said good-bye to her in a very friendly way, and he gave me what I asked for bringing her up here without any haggling, and something over as well. She has been well treated, wherever she's been, and has come home of her own accord." These little bits of news spread so rapidly that before nightfall every house in the village knew that Heidi had left a good home in Frankfurt to come back, of her own accord, to her grandfather.

As soon as she got away from the people, Heidi rushed uphill as fast as she could go. She had to stop every now and then to get her breath, for her basket was heavy and the mountain slope steep, but she had only one thought: "Will Grannie still be sitting in the corner by her spinning wheel? Oh, I hope she hasn't died." Then she saw the little house in the hollow, and her heart beat faster than ever. She raced up to the door but could hardly open it, she was trembling so much, but she managed it, and flew into the little room quite out of breath and unable to say a word.

> 66 As soon as she got away from the people, Heidi rushed uphill as fast as she could go. 99

"Goodness me," someone said from the corner of the room, "that was how Heidi used to come in! How I wish she would come and see me again. Who is it?"

"It's Heidi, Grannie," she cried, and threw herself onto the old woman's lap and hugged her, too overcome with happiness to say anything more. And at first Grannie was so surprised, she could not speak either, but just stroked Heidi's head. Then she murmured, "Yes, it's Heidi's curly hair and her voice. Praise God she's come back to us." A few big tears fell from her old blind eyes onto Heidi's hand. "It's really you, child."

"Yes, really and truly, Grannie. Don't cry," said Heidi. "I'm here and I'll never go away again. I'll come and see you every day. And you won't have to eat hard bread for a few days, Grannie," she added, and she brought out the rolls one by one and laid them on Grannie's lap.

"Child, what a present to bring me!" exclaimed the old woman, as her hands moved over the load on her lap. "But you're the best present of all." And she stroked Heidi's hot cheeks. "Say something, anything at all, just to let me hear your voice."

"I was so afraid you might have died while I was away," said Heidi, "then I would never have seen you again, and you wouldn't have had the rolls."

Peter's mother came in at this moment and stared in amazement when she saw Heidi. "Fancy you here," she said at last, "and she's wearing such a pretty dress, Grannie. She looks so fine I hardly recognized her. And a little hat with a feather—I suppose that is yours too. Put it on and let me see you in it."

"No, I won't," said Heidi very decidedly. "You can have that. I don't want it any more. I've got my old one." And she opened her red bundle and there it was, more battered than ever after the journey, but that didn't worry her. She had never forgotten her grandfather saying that he would not like to see her in a hat with a feather, and that was why she had taken such care of the old one, for she had always counted on going back to him.

"That's silly," said Bridget. "I can't possibly take it from you. It's a

For those who lived in the Alps during Heidi's time, raising livestock was the chief profession. The milk produced by animals grazing in the mountains was of such high quality that excellent butter and cheeses could be made from it. To a lesser extent, the animals also provided meat.

very smart hat, and if you really don't want it, perhaps the schoolmaster's daughter would buy it from you." Heidi said no more, but put the hat away in a corner out of sight. Then she took off her pretty dress, and put the old red scarf on over her petticoat.

"Good-bye, Grannie. I must go on to Grandfather now, but I'll come and see you again tomorrow."

Grannie hugged her as if she could not bear to let her go.

"Why have you taken off your pretty frock?" asked Bridget.

"I'd rather go to Grandfather like this, otherwise he might not recognize me. You hardly knew me in it."

Bridget went outside with her. "You could have kept it on," she said, "he'd have known you all right. But you be careful. Peter says Uncle Alp is so bad-tempered now, and never speaks to him."

Heidi said good-bye and went on her way. The evening sun shone rosily on the mountains, and she kept turning round to look at them, for they lay behind her as she climbed. Everything seemed even more beautiful than she had expected. The twin peaks of Falkniss, snow-covered Scesaplana, the pasture land, and the valley below were all red and gold, and there were little pink clouds floating in the sky. It was so lovely, Heidi stood with tears pouring down her

66 She threw herself onto the old woman's lap and hugged her, too overcome with happiness to say anything more. And at first Grannie was so surprised, she could not speak either, but just stroked Heidi's head.**99**

cheeks, and thanked God for letting her come home to it again. She could find no words to express her feelings, but lingered until the light began to fade and then ran on. Soon she could see the tops of the fir trees, then the roof, then the whole hut and last Grandfather himself, sitting on the bench outside and smoking his pipe, just as he used to do. Before he had time to see who it was, she had dropped her basket on the ground and flung her arms around him, crying, "Grandfather, Grandfather." She could say no more, and he couldn't speak at all. For the first time in years, his eyes were wet with tears and he had to brush his hand over them. Then he loosened her arms from his neck and set her on his knee.

" It was so lovely, Heidi stood with tears pouring down her cheeks, and thanked God for letting her come home to it again. "

"So you've come back, Heidi," he said. "Why's that, eh? And you don't look so very grand either. Did they send you away?"

"Oh no, Grandfather, don't think that. Clara and her father and Grandmamma were all very kind to me. But I was very homesick. I used to get a lump in my throat, as if I was choking. But I didn't say anything, because they would have thought I was not grateful. Then suddenly Mr. Sesemann called me very early one morning—but I think the doctor had something to do with it. Oh, I expect it's all in the letter." She jumped down and ran to fetch the letter and the fat packet.

"The packet is for you," he said, laying it on the bench. Then he read the letter and put it in his pocket without a word.

"Do you think you could drink some milk, Heidi?" he asked, preparing to go indoors with her. "Bring the packet with you. There's money in it for you to buy a bed and any clothes you may need."

"I don't want it," said Heidi gaily. "I've got a bed already, and Clara gave me so many clothes I'm sure I shall never want any more."

"Bring it in all the same, and put it in the cupboard," said Uncle Alp. "You'll find a use for it one day."

Fir trees grow well in nearly any kind of soil, but are susceptible to drought. They thrive in rich, well-watered ground and do best on slopes with a northern exposure. When the trees grow old, their silhouettes become narrower and they lose their lowest branches.

Heidi brought it indoors. She looked round eagerly at everything, then climbed up to the loft. "Oh, my bed's gone," she cried, very disappointed.

"We can soon make it again," he called up. "I didn't know you'd be coming back. Now come and have some milk."

She sat down on her old high chair and drained her mug as though she had never tasted anything so delicious in her life. Then she drew a deep breath and said, "There's nothing as good as our milk anywhere in the world."

There came a shrill whistle then, and Heidi shot

out of the door to see Peter coming down the path, surrounded by his lively goats. When he caught sight of her, he stopped dead and stared in astonishment.

"Hullo, Peter," she called and ran toward him. "Oh, there's Daisy and Dusky. Do you remember me?" They did indeed seem to recognize her voice, and rubbed their heads against her, bleating. She called the other goats by name and they all came crowding round her. Impatient Finch jumped clean over two other animals to reach her, and even shy Snowflake pressed forward and butted big Turk to one side. Turk was very surprised and tossed his head as if to say, "Look what you're doing!" Heidi was delighted to see them all again. She put an arm round one and patted another. The animals pushed her this way and that with their affectionate nudgings, but at last she came to Peter's side.

"Aren't you going to say hello to me?" she asked.

He recovered himself then and said, "So you're back again," adding, as he always used to in the old days, "Coming up with me tomorrow?"

"Not tomorrow, but perhaps the day after. I must go and see Grannie tomorrow."

"I'm glad you're back," he said, with a wide grin, and prepared to move on, but he found it very difficult

The alpenhorn, a Swiss musical instrument, is carved out of fir. Its powerful tone allowed herders to communicate at a distance and call their flocks in. The unusual acoustical conditions at high altitudes enhance the instrument's sweet and resonant timbre.

to get the goats together again. He called and scolded, but as soon as he had gathered them round him, they all turned to follow Heidi who was taking Daisy and Dusky towards their stall, with an arm thrown round each. She had to go right inside with them and shut the door, before Peter could get the rest of the herd on the move.

When she went indoors again she found her grandfather had made her a lovely sweet-smelling bed, with hay which had not long been gathered in, and had covered it comfortably with clean linen sheets. When she lay down in it a little later, she slept as she had not done all the time she had been away.

66 He couldn't speak at all. For the first time in years, his eyes were wet with tears.**99**

During the night Uncle Alp went up to the loft at least ten times to make sure she was all right, and to

see that the round hole in the wall was still stopped with hay to prevent the moonlight shining on her face. But Heidi did not stir. She slept soundly all night long, satisfied through and through. She was home again. She had seen the sun setting on the mountains. She had heard the wind whistling through the fir trees.

'There's nothing as good as our milk anywhere in the world.'

14

WHEN THE CHURCH BELLS RING

Heidi stood under the swaying trees, waiting for her grandfather to go down the mountain with her. He was going to fetch her trunk from Dörfli while she visited Grannie. She was eager to get there, to hear how she had enjoyed the rolls but, listening to the familiar rustling of the trees with her eyes resting on the distant green pastures, she did not grow impatient.

Presently he came out of the hut and took a last

Inside this mountain chalet, a pile of logs and kindling rests on two beams over the hearth to dry out. Firewood must be very dry in order not to fill the room with smoke.

look round. It was Saturday, the day when he always cleaned the whole place, inside and out, and tidied up generally. He had worked hard all the morning so that he would be free to go with Heidi in the afternoon, and now everything looked spick and span so he could leave it with a clear conscience. "Now we can go," he said.

They parted company outside the little house where Peter lived, and Heidi went in there. Grannie heard her step at once, and called affectionately, "Is that you, child?" She took Heidi's hand and held it tightly as if she was afraid of losing her again.

"How did you like the rolls?" asked Heidi at once.

"Oh, they taste good! I feel better already."

"Grannie's so anxious to make them last that she would only eat one last night and another this morning," put in Bridget. "If she has one every day for the next ten days, I'm sure she'll get back her strength."

Heidi listened thoughtfully and an idea came to her. "I know what I'll do, Grannie," she cried. "I'll write to Clara. I'm sure she'll send me more rolls. I'd saved lots and lots for you, but they were all thrown away, and then Clara promised she'd give me as many as I wanted. She'll keep her word, I know."

"That's a kind thought," said Bridget, "but I'm afraid they'd be quite stale and hard by the time they got here. If I had a spare copper or two I'd get some from the baker in Dörfli, but it's as much as I can do to buy the black bread."

A beaming smile spread over Heidi's face. "But I've got lots of money, Grannie," she exclaimed, "and now I know what I can do with it. You shall have a fresh roll every day and two on Sundays, and Peter can bring them up with him from the village."

"No, no," protested Grannie, "you mustn't spend your money on me. You give it to Grandfather, and he'll tell you what to do with it."

Heidi paid no attention but pranced round the room, singing, "Now Grannie can have a fresh roll every day and will soon be strong again! And oh Grannie, when you're quite well, surely you'll be able to see too. It's probably only because you're so weak that you can't see."

Grannie just smiled. She would not spoil the child's happiness. As she danced around, Heidi caught sight of Grannie's old hymn book, and that gave her another idea. "I can read now, Grannie," she said. "Would you like me to read you something out of your old book?"

"Oh, yes," exclaimed Grannie, delighted. "Can you really read?"

Heidi climbed on a stool and

The main room in a chalet serves as a combination kitchen, dining room, and bedroom. All the work of the household is done there, and it is the focus of family life. This chalet, which has quite comfortable furniture, is equipped with beds that can be curtained off from the rest of the room by heavy drapery.

took down the book, which had lain on the shelf so long that it was thick with dust. She wiped it clean and took the stool close beside the old woman. "What shall I read?" she asked.

"What you like, child," Grannie said, pushing her spinning wheel to one side and waiting eagerly for her to begin.

Heidi turned the pages, reading a line here and a line there. "Here's one about the sun," she said at last. "I'll read that." And she began with great enthusiasm.

> "The golden sun
> His course doth run,
> And spreads his light,
> So warm and bright,
> Upon us all.
>
> "We see God's power
> From hour to hour.
> His love is sure,
> And will endure
> For evermore.
>
> "Sorrow and grief
> Are only brief.
> True joy we'll find,
> And peace of mind,
> In God's good time."

Grannie sat through it with her hands folded. Heidi had never seen her look so happy, though tears were running down her cheeks. And at the end she said, "Read it again, Heidi. Please read it again."

Heidi was delighted to do so for she liked the hymn very much herself.

"Oh, that's done me so much good," Grannie sighed at last. "It makes my old heart rejoice."

Heidi had never seen such a peaceful expression before on Grannie's careworn face. It looked as though she had indeed found "true joy and peace of mind."

Then there came a knock on the window and Heidi saw her grandfather outside, beckoning to her. She said good-bye and promised to come again next day. "I may go to the pasture with Peter and the goats in the morning," she added, "but I'll be here in the afternoon." It had been pleasant to be able to give so much happiness, and Heidi wanted to do that even more than running on the mountain among the flowers with the goats.

The many varieties of cows in the Alps are bred for their milk production. Those from the Val d'Herens take part each year in an unusual contest: wearing heavy bells, they are pitted against each other in single combat, though the bouts are more colorful than violent. The winner is declared "Queen of the Cows."

This shepherd's hut is a simple dwelling dug into the side of a mountain. It consists of flat stones and wooden beams primitively joined.

As she was going Bridget brought out the dress and hat which Heidi had taken off and left behind the day before. Now she thought she might as well take the dress, for she was sure it would not make any difference to Grandfather, but the hat she absolutely refused. "You keep that," she told Bridget. "I'll never wear it again."

Heidi had so much to tell her grandfather that she began at once.

"And I'd like to buy rolls for Grannie with my money," she told him. "She doesn't want me to, but it'll be all right, won't it? Peter can get them in Dörfli, if I give him a penny every day, and two on Sunday."

"What about your bed, Heidi? It would be nice for you to have a proper one, and there would still be enough money to buy the rolls."

"But I sleep much better on my hay mattress than I did in that great big bed in Frankfurt. Please, please let me spend the money on rolls."

"Well," he agreed at last, "the money is yours. Do what you like with it. There'll be enough to buy Grannie rolls for many a long year."

"Good, good! She needn't ever eat the hard black bread again. Oh, we are having good times, Grandfather, aren't we?" and she skipped gaily along beside him. Then all at once she grew serious and said, "If God had let me come back to you at once, like I asked in my prayers, none of this would have happened. I should have brought Grannie a few rolls I had saved, but they would soon have been gone, and I wouldn't have been able to read. God knew what was best, just as Clara's Grandmamma said He did, and see how perfectly He arranged everything. I'll always say my prayers after this, as Grandmamma told me to, and if God doesn't answer them at once I shall know it's because He's planning something better for me, just as He did in Frankfurt. We'll pray every day, won't we Grandfather, and we'll never forget God again, and He won't forget us."

"And when someone does forget?" he said softly.

"That's very bad," Heidi told him earnestly, "because then God lets him go his own way and then, when everything has gone wrong, no one will feel sorry for him. They'll only say, 'You didn't bother about God, and now God has left you to yourself.'"

"That's true, Heidi. How did you find out?"

"Grandmamma explained it all to me."

The old man walked on in silence. After a while he said, half to himself, "If God forsakes a man, that's final. There's no going back then."

"Oh, but there is. Grandmamma said so, and everything will come right in the end, like it does in the lovely story in my book. You haven't heard it yet, but we'll soon be home now, and then I'll read it to you." Heidi hurried as fast as she could go up the last

Saint Nicholas, whose feast day is celebrated by Catholics on the sixth of December, was extremely popular in the Middle Ages and became known as "the Christmas man." He was often depicted as bringing presents to children. There is a legend that he once brought three children back to life who had been killed by a butcher.

steep slope, and when they reached the hut, she let go his hand and ran indoors. He took the basket off his back. He had packed half the contents of her trunk in it, for the whole thing would have been too heavy for him to carry so far uphill. Then he sat down on the bench outside, lost in thought, until Heidi reappeared with the book under her arm. "That's good, you're all ready," she said, climbing onto the seat beside him.

She had read the story so often that the book opened at the right place by itself, and she began straightaway to read about the young man with the shepherd's crook and the fine cloak, who looked after his father's sheep and goats in the fields. "One day," she continued, "he asked for his share of his father's fortune so that he might go away and be his own master. As soon as he got it, he left home and wasted it all. When it was gone, he had to go and work for his living, and he got a job with a farmer, who had no flocks nor pastures as his father had, but only pigs. This young man had to look after them. His fine clothes were gone, and he had only rags to cover him, and only the pigs' swill to eat, and he was very sad when he remembered how well he had been treated at home, and realized how ungrateful he had been to his father. Alone with the pigs, he wept with remorse and homesickness and thought, 'I will rise up and go to my father and ask

During the time *Heidi* takes place, many of the Zurich townspeople boated across the lake on Sundays to hear the priest of the island of Ufenau give his sermon in front of the rustic little parish church.

him to forgive me. I will say to him that I am no longer worthy to be treated as his son, but ask if he will let me be one of his servants.' So he set out, and when he was still a long way off, his father saw him and came running toward him." Heidi broke off to ask, "What do you suppose happens now? I expect you think his father would be angry and say, 'I told you so.' Just you listen though. When his father saw him, his heart was filled with compassion for him, and he ran and met him and put his arms round him and kissed him; and his son said, 'Father, I have done wrong against Heaven and against you and am no longer worthy to be your son.' But his father called to the servants, 'Bring me the good robe and put it on him, and a ring for his finger and shoes for his feet. Fetch the calf we have fattened and kill it for a feast, and we will eat and be merry, for this my son was dead to me and is alive again, he was lost and is found.' And they began to be merry."

66 She had read the story so often that the book opened at the right place by itself. 99

Instead of looking pleased and surprised as she had expected, the old man sat very still, without speaking, until she said, "Isn't that a lovely story, Grandfather?"

"It is indeed," he replied, but he looked so grave that she too fell silent, and sat looking at the pictures. Presently she pushed the book gently in front of him. "You can see how happy he is," she said, pointing to the picture of the return of the prodigal son.

Some hours later, when Heidi was in bed and asleep, the old man climbed up to the loft and put his lamp on the ground so that its light fell on her. She lay with her hands folded, as if she had fallen asleep saying her prayers. There was a peaceful, very trusting expression on her face, which moved him deeply and he stood gazing down at her for a long time. Then he too folded his hands, bowed his head, and, in a low voice, said, "Father, I have sinned against Heaven and before Thee and am no longer worthy to be called Thy son," and down his wrinkled cheeks rolled two large tears.

He rose early next morning and went out of doors. It was a beautiful day—a Sunday. The sound of bells floated up from the valley and the birds in the fir trees were singing their morning chorus. Then he stepped back into the hut and called up to Heidi, "Time to get up. The sun is shining. Put on your best dress and we'll go to church together."

A mass in Bern, Switzerland. Sunday mass is an important ritual in the Catholic religion. The church bells ring, inviting the faithful to come to service.

She had never heard him suggest such a thing before, and she soon came hurrying down, wearing one of the pretty Frankfurt dresses. At sight of him, she stopped in astonishment.

"I've never seen you dressed like that before, Grandfather," she exclaimed. "Silver buttons on your jacket. You do look fine in your Sunday clothes."

He smiled at her. "And so do you," he said. "Now let's go." He took her hand and together they set off down the steep path. Bells from many churches were ringing, getting louder and clearer as grandfather and child went on, and the joyful clanging delighted Heidi.

"Oh, Grandfather, this must be a very special day," she cried.

The people of Dörfli were already in church and the singing had started as Heidi and Uncle Alp went in and sat down at the back. The hymn was hardly over before people were nudging one another and whispering that Uncle Alp was in church. Women kept turning round to look and so lost the place in their hymn-books, and the leader of the choir simply could not keep the voices together. But when the pastor began to preach, everyone gave him their attention, for he spoke of praise and thanksgiving, and with such warmth that his listeners were truly moved.

At the end of the service the old man took Heidi by the hand again, and they went toward the pastor's house. The congregation watched them with interest. Several people followed to see whether they would actually go inside and, when they did so, hung around in little groups, asking what it could possibly mean and speculating whether Uncle Alp would come out

The clothes worn by these young Swiss girls were very likely reserved for special occasions, such as going to church. Their outfits included brightly embroidered bonnets with gold and silver thread, shawls and aprons decorated with needlework, and flounced skirts.

again angry or friendly. There were those who said, "He can't be as bad as people make out. Did you see how gently he held the child by the hand?" or "I've always said they were wrong! He wouldn't be going to see the pastor at all if he was such a bad lot."

"What did I tell you?" demanded the baker. "Would the child have left that place where she was so well looked after, with plenty to eat and drink, and

66 'I've never seen you dressed like that before, Grandfather. You do look fine in your Sunday clothes.'99

196

have come back, of her own accord, to him if he was as hard and bad as people said?" Gradually they all changed their minds about old Uncle Alp and began to feel quite friendly toward him. Then some women joined in the talk, and they had heard from Bridget and Grannie how Uncle Alp had come down and patched up their cottage for them and stopped the shutters rattling; and in no time, they were looking eagerly at the house door, like old friends waiting to welcome home a traveler who had been long away, and greatly missed.

This rounded bell tower sits atop a square turret with a large clock face on each side. Above it rises a six-sided spire made of wood and covered with lead, inside which is the church bell.

Now when Uncle Alp had gone inside the pastor's house, he knocked on the study door and the pastor came out, looking quite as though he had expected the visit—for of course he had seen them in church. He shook hands with Uncle Alp so warmly that at first the lonely old man could hardly speak. He had not expected such kindness. When he had collected himself, he said:

"I've come to ask you to forget what I said when you called on me that time, and not to hold it against me that I wouldn't take your friendly advice. You were quite right and I was wrong. I shall do as you suggested and move down to Dörfli for the winter. The weather is too severe then for the child to be up in the hut. And if the people down here do regard me with suspicion, that's no more than I deserve; and I know *you* won't do so."

The pastor's face showed how pleased he was. He pressed Uncle Alp's hand again, and said, "Neighbor, your mountains have been a good church to you, and brought you to mine in the right frame of mind. You've made me very happy. You'll never regret coming back to live among us, I'm sure. And as for myself, I shall always welcome you as a dear friend and neighbor, and I look forward to our spending many pleasant winter evenings together. And we'll find friends for Heidi too," he added, putting his hand on her curly head. He went with them to the door, and all the people outside saw them part like old friends. As soon as the door was closed everybody crowded round Uncle Alp with outstretched hands, each wishing to be the first to greet him, so that he

66 He went with them to the door, and all the people outside saw them part like old friends. **99**

didn't know where to begin. "We're so pleased to see you among us again," they said; or "I've long been wanting to have a chat with you, Uncle." Such greetings were heard on every side, and when he 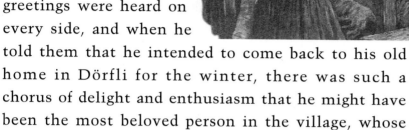 told them that he intended to come back to his old home in Dörfli for the winter, there was such a chorus of delight and enthusiasm that he might have been the most beloved person in the village, whose absence had been keenly felt by everyone.

In the nineteenth century and in the beginning of the twentieth, it was rare for a child to be raised solely by his or her parents. An important part of a child's upbringing consisted in having an extended family circle, which typically included grandparents, aunts and uncles, and cousins. In contrast, the boundaries of today's nuclear families are more narrowly drawn.

When he and Heidi started for home at last, many people went part of the way with them, and when they finally said good-bye, they begged him to visit them in their homes before long. As he watched them go, Heidi saw such a kind light in his eye, that she said, "Grandfather, you look quite different—nicer and nicer. I've never seen you so before."

"No," he replied. "You see, today I am happy, as I had never thought to be again. Much happier than I deserve. It's good to feel at peace with God and man. It was a good day when God sent you to me."

When they reached Peter's cottage, he opened the door and went in. "Good day, Grannie," he called. "I can see I must get busy with some more repairs before the autumn winds begin to blow."

"Goodness me, is it Uncle Alp?" cried the old woman. "What a fine surprise. Now I can thank you for all you did for us before. May God reward you."

She held out her hand, which trembled a little, and he shook it heartily. "I've something in my heart, I'd like to say to you," she went on. "If I've ever done you any harm, don't punish me by letting Heidi go away again, while I'm still above ground. You don't know what she means to me," and she hugged Heidi, whose arms were already round her neck.

"Don't worry, Grannie," Uncle replied reassuringly, "I won't punish either of us in that way. We'll all be together now, and for some time yet, please God."

Bridget took Uncle aside then to show him the hat with the feather, and told him that Heidi had said she could keep it, but that she really couldn't take it from the child. Uncle Alp gave Heidi an approving look. "That hat is hers, and if she doesn't want to wear it, she's right. You should certainly keep it since she's given it to you."

Bridget was delighted. Holding the hat up, she exclaimed, "Just fancy, it must be worth quite a lot of money. How well Heidi got on in Frankfurt. I wonder if it would be any good sending Peter there for a while. What do you think, Uncle?"

His eyes twinkled. "It certainly wouldn't do him any harm, but opportunity's a great thing."

At that moment Peter himself came charging in, out of breath, and banged his head against the door in his haste. He held out a letter for Heidi which he had been given at the post office. No one had letters in his home, and Heidi had certainly never had one before. Everybody sat down and listened while she opened it, and read it aloud. It was from Clara, who wrote:

"It's been so dreadfully dull here since you went away, that I can hardly bear it. But Papa has promised me that I can go to Ragaz in the autumn. Grandmamma will come with me. After that she says we may come to visit you and your grandfather. I told her about you wanting to take some rolls to Grannie, and she was pleased, and said I was to tell you you were quite right. She is sending some coffee for her to have with them, and says she would like to see Grannie as well when we come to the mountains."

Not all middle-class children had a tutor or governess. Sometimes the older children taught the younger to read and write. In a time before radio, television, or computers, reading books (sometimes illustrated with beautiful engravings) was a favorite form of entertainment.

Everyone was interested in Clara's news, and they talked about it so long that not even Uncle noticed how late it was getting. Then again, they had had much to say about the pleasure of Uncle's visit, and the promise of more to come.

"It feels good to have you here again, old friend, after such a long time," Grannie said. "It gives me faith that one day we'll all be together with those we love. Do come again soon, and Heidi, you'll be here tomorrow?"

They both assured her that they would, and then said good-bye. All the church bells around were ringing for evening prayer as they went back up the mountain, and they found the hut bathed in the glow of the setting sun.

The prospect of Clara's Grandmamma coming there in the autumn gave Heidi plenty to think about. She had seen, at Frankfurt, that when that lady came upon the scene, she had a way of making everything run happily and smoothly.

66 'Grandfather, you look quite different—nicer and nicer. I've never seen you so before.'
'No,' he replied. 'You see, today I am happy, as I had never thought to be again. It's good to feel at peace with God and man. It was a good day when God sent you to me.'**99**

A Note on the Text

The book that most people today know simply as *Heidi* was originally published in two separate volumes. In 1880, *Heidis Lehr- und Wanderjahre (Heidi's Years of Wandering and Learning)* was published in Gotha, Germany. The book, which begins with Heidi meeting her grandfather and ends with her joyous return from Frankfurt, was an immediate success. The following year brought *Heidi kann brauchen, was es gelernt hat (Heidi Makes Use of What She Has Learned)*, which deals with the visit of the invalid Clara and her grandmother, and Clara's miraculous recovery. This book too was immensely popular.

The first English translation was published in London in 1884; it appeared in two volumes, *Heidi's Early Experiences* and *Heidi's Further Experiences*. That same year a translation was published in Boston in a single volume called *Heidi, Her Years of Wandering and Learning*. Since that time many more editions have been published all over the world, as *Heidi* swiftly achieved and continues to maintain its place as a beloved classic of international children's literature. In addition, several films have been made about Heidi, most notably a version featuring the child star Shirley Temple in 1937. In 1958 two sequels to the original story, *Heidi Grows Up* and *Heidi's Children*, were published by Charles Tritten, one of the many translators of the book.

ILLUSTRATION CREDITS

Éditions Gallimard

Director: Pierre Marchand
Editor: Cécile Dutheil de la Rochère
Illustrations: Brigitte Célerier, Sophie Fougère
Layout: Chita-Geneviève Lévy
Proofreading: Béatrice Peyret-Vignals, Evelyne Pezzopane

Viking

Editor: Lisa Bernstein
Design: Nina Putignano
Production Editor: Janet Pascal

VIKING
Published by the Penguin Group
Penguin Books USA Inc., 375 Hudson Street, New York, New York 10014, U.S.A.
Penguin Books Ltd, 27 Wrights Lane, London W8 5TZ, England
Penguin Books Australia Ltd, Ringwood, Victoria, Australia
Penguin Books Canada Ltd, 10 Alcorn Avenue, Toronto, Ontario, Canada M4V 3B2
Penguin Books (N.Z.) Ltd, 182–190 Wairau Road, Auckland 10, New Zealand

Penguin Books Ltd, Registered Offices: Harmondsworth, Middlesex, England

First published in 1880

This English translation published in 1956 in Great Britain by Penguin Books Ltd.
This illustrated edition published in 1995 in France by Éditions Gallimard

Published in 1996 in the United States of America by Viking, a division of Penguin Books USA Inc.

Simultaneously published in a hardcover edition

3 5 7 9 10 8 6 4 2

Translation copyright © Penguin Books Ltd, 1956
Copyright © Éditions Gallimard, 1994
All rights reserved

Translated from the German by Eileen Hall
Illustrations by Rozier-Gaudriault
Captions by Ariane Chottin and Antoine Guémy
Note translation by Willard Wood

ISBN 0-670-86987-2

Printed in Italy
Set in Trump Mediaeval